FIVE RE~~A~~ ✔ KU-016-415 ~~'LL~~ LO~~VE THIS BOO~~K

(ACCORDING TO STAN)

EXPERT TIPS and ADVICE on how to survive little brothers (or sisters!)

Cool SPACE FACTS

Really funny **CHARTS**, **GRAPHS**, and **TABLES**!

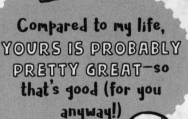

Compared to my life, YOURS IS PROBABLY PRETTY GREAT—so that's good (for you anyway!)

HILARIOUS (yeah, right) bits ~~about bodies and wee (if~~

STAN'S WORLD
GEMMA
WANT
SCIENCE
SCHOOL
KNOW
fair
KIT
CAKE
time
FLOSSIE
DAD
ROOM
MUM
GOOD
TODAY
FRED
recipe
BRUV
WOW
SORRY
GRAN
MOON
REALIZE
NOW
SWAT
LIAM
WEIRD
JESS
BROTHER
SOLAR
bed
LEVELS
UM
HELP
IMPOSSIBLE
FRIENDS
FAMILY
FOX
NEED
METEORITE
EAT
PEOPLE
SPACE
EARTH
right
LIFE
YOUNGER
EMBARRASSMENT
TELESCOPE
CATASTROPHE

FOR GEORGE AND ALEX

OXFORD
UNIVERSITY PRESS

Great Clarendon Street, Oxford OX2 6DP

Oxford University Press is a department of the University of Oxford.
It furthers the University's objective of excellence in research, scholarship,
and education by publishing worldwide. Oxford is a registered trade mark
of Oxford University Press in the UK and in certain other countries

Text copyright © Elaine Wickson 2018
Ilustration copyright © Chris Judge 2018
Decorative artwork by Shutterstock

The moral rights of the author have been asserted

Database right Oxford University Press (maker)

First published 2018

British Library Cataloguing in Publication Data

Data available

ISBN: 978-0-19-275904-7

1 3 5 7 9 10 8 6 4 2

Printed in Great Britain

Paper used in the production of this book is a natural,
recyclable product made from wood grown in sustainable forests.
The manufacturing process conforms to the environmental
regulations of the country of origin.

PLANET STAN

STAN
MY LIFE
IN PIE CHARTS

(OR THE ULTIMATE GUIDE TO SURVIVING BROTHERS)

ELAINE WICKSON
PICTURES BY CHRIS JUDGE

OXFORD
UNIVERSITY PRESS

⤷ BRUVHOOD

'Mum! Fred's been keeping snails under my bed again . . .'

They say we're all made of stardust. Your toes. A badger. Even a Twix. Everything in the universe is made from the same stuff. Well, not _EVERYTHING_. My younger brother definitely isn't. He's seventy per cent annoying and thirty per cent fart.

I'm not sure he knows how to be a brother. Like when he turned my **PLANETS OF THE SOLAR SYSTEM POSTER** into a **BOGIES OF THE SOLAR SYSTEM POSTER**. Or the time he put a family of ladybirds in my lunchbox. Or the day he threw all my pants out the window just as Jess McGregor walked by, including the pair with space rockets on.

MY GENERAL STATE OF MIND

OVER THE MOON

SUNNY

CALM

OK

PHEW

NOT OK

ALARMED

NEED CAKE

STORMY

BLACK HOLE OF DOOM

(7)

Dad says: 'YOUR BROTHER KNOWS EXACTLY
HOW TO BE A BROTHER, STANLEY. THAT
BEHAVIOUR IS WELL WITHIN THE NORMAL
PARAMETERS OF BROTHERHOOD.'

> **Brotherhood** The relationship between brothers.
> A feeling of friendship, support, and understanding.

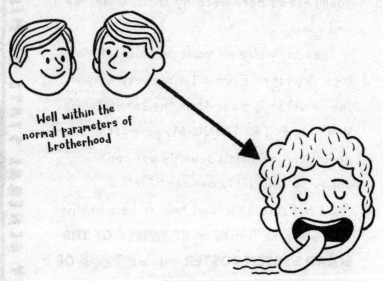

Well within the
normal parameters of
brotherhood

My brother stood so far outside the
parameters of brotherhood, he's entered into
his own warped dimension where licking the
cake shop window is acceptable behaviour

At no point in the definition does it say: THE
YOUNGER SIBLING ABSOLUTELY HAS TO BE
IN JUST HIS PANTS WHENEVER YOUR MATES

CALL ROUND. OH, AND CHECK UNDER YOUR
BED FOR WILDLIFE.

'D'you think they're too big for the Hoover?'
Mum sighs heavily at the prospect of
de-snailing our room.

The only way she can cope with Fred's antics
is with <u>MUM O'CLOCK</u> at the end of each day,
which involves watching loads of EastEnders.

'Are you sure we have to share a room?' I
ask her as we watch the gastropod molluscs
slowly leave a trail over my SKY AT NIGHT
POSTER, creating new constellations as
they climb. 'What about the landing cupboard?
He could sleep upright like the astronauts on
the International Space Station.'

'He can't sleep upright, he's your brother.'

Well that's no excuse.

There are at least a hundred billion
planets in the MILKY WAY. How come
I ended up on the same planet as Fred?
Mum says he's an effervescent life force.
An effervescent life force
doesn't put toothpaste in your

MY GENERAL STATE OF MIND

OVER THE MOON
SUNNY
CALM
OK
PHEW
NOT OK
ALARMED
NEED CAKE
STORMY
BLACK HOLE OF DOOM

slippers. An annoying life force does that.

'You have to take the rough with the smooth,' Mum explains, picking snails off the walls.

She's always quoting her bonkers fridge magnets to try and convince me having a brother is worth it.

Why can't life be like my **1001 SPACE FACTS BOOK**? If a few nifty illustrations can help explain a solar eclipse then why not how to understand Freds? There's always one hanging about at your ninth birthday party who would rather play pin the *BOGEY* on the donkey. Or make the entire buffet null and void at your tenth birthday party by licking all the crisps and putting them back again. Or running about completely starkers at your eleventh birthday party shouting

I'M WEE WILLIE WINKIE!

so your mates up and leave because they need to wash their eyes (and hang on a minute, didn't Wee Willie Winkie run about in *AT LEAST* a nightgown?) Fred should definitely come with diagrams.

I'd like a diagram to help explain why Mum called me `STANLEY` `WINSTON` `FOX.` You'd think I'd been named after an ancient great-grandfather with a name like that, wouldn't you? But no. Mum travelled back in time to the eighteen hundreds to find a name buried in an archaeological dig of ridiculous names they hoped nobody would ever dig up again, and then came back to the future to give it to me.

Parents should lay off calling their babies anything until they're old enough to choose their own. Or admit they've got it wrong, like they did with <u>URANUS</u>—a planet that was originally called George and probably wishes it still was. I should have had a cool spacethemed name, especially as I have seven freckles on my right cheek shaped like the <u>PLOUGH</u>. Which people love to point out to me all the time, even though
<u>IT'S ON MY FACE.</u>

MY GENERAL STATE OF MIND

OVER THE MOON
SUNNY
CALM
OK
PHEW
NOT OK
ALARMED
NEED CAKE
STORMY
BLACK HOLE of DOOM

My younger brother fared slightly better on the name front: FREDERICK ALBERT FOX. Pretty apt his initials spell FAF seeing as that's what he spends a hundred per cent of his time doing.

FAFFING ABOUT
ACHIEVED BY FRED THIS WEEK

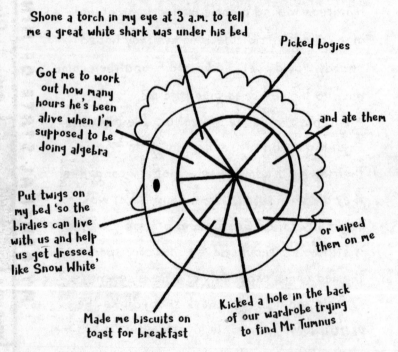

Shone a torch in my eye at 3 a.m. to tell me a great white shark was under his bed

Picked bogies

Got me to work out how many hours he's been alive when I'm supposed to be doing algebra

and ate them

Put twigs on my bed 'so the birdies can live with us and help us get dressed like Snow White'

or wiped them on me

Made me biscuits on toast for breakfast

Kicked a hole in the back of our wardrobe trying to find Mr Tumnus

'Can we be brothers for ever, Stan?' Fred dashes in, ignoring the snail chaos, and trampolining on my bed whilst scoffing toast to make sure there are more crumbs than duvet left on my bed.

'Well yeah. Dur.'

Because we actually ARE brothers. Have been since he was born. And did I have a say in this? No. All of a sudden I was expected to share my parents (and by share I mean not share at all):

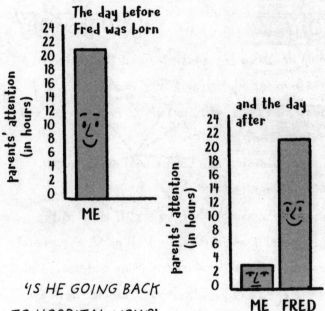

The day before Fred was born

Parents' attention (in hours)

24 22 20 18 16 14 12 10 8 6 4 2 0

ME

and the day after

Parents' attention (in hours)

24 22 20 18 16 14 12 10 8 6 4 2 0

ME   FRED

'IS HE GOING BACK TO HOSPITAL NOW?'

I enquired politely on Day Two.

'OF COURSE NOT STANLEY, HE'S GOING TO BRING JOY TO OUR LIVES FOR EVER.'

OVER THE MOON

SUNNY

CALM

OK

PHEW

NOT OK

ALARMED

NEED CAKE

STORMY

BLACK HOLE OF DOOM

MY GENERAL STATE OF MIND

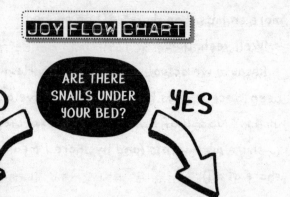

ARE THERE SNAILS UNDER YOUR BED?

NO

YES

JOY

NOT JOY

Mum holds up the missing salad that's been stashed under my bed with a slug still attached. 'Snails I can cope with, but slugs—what were you thinking, Fred?'

'Squelchy didn't want to be left alone in the puddle,' he pouts.

'Squelchy's going to wish he still WAS in the puddle after I've finished with him. Now go fetch your father from the garden,' Mum orders.

While Fred's out of the room I decide to take advantage of the situation. If you're ever going to ask your parents for anything, do it when your younger bruv infests your room with snails.

'Things I have to put up with eh?' I tut. 'And he

destroyed the **DEATH STAR** last night.'

Obviously not the *ACTUAL* imperial battle station a long time ago in a galaxy, far, far away, but my Lego version.

'I know, pea-pod,' Mum draws me in for a hug. 'But we'll soon fix it.'

I admire my mother's optimism but there's nothing north of the basement.

'Soooo, I was wondering . . .' I take a deep breath. 'Can I have a telescope? Because you've got Mum o'clock and Dad's got his shed, while I'm still upstairs with Fred and his bogies. It's the least I deserve.'

I've been after a telescope since I was a small-year-old. I thought I'd got one at the age of seven, when I excitedly opened a present from my parents. Turned out to be a crazy golf set.

'Is it sensible to keep Fred and a telescope in the same room?' asks Mum, leaning her head on mine. 'A house of inexpensive

MY GENERAL STATE OF MIND

OVER THE MOON
SUNNY
CALM
OK
PHEW
NOT OK
ALARMED
NEED CAKE
STORMY
BLACK HOLE OF DOOM

things is just BASIC FRED-PROOFING.'

I guess she's got a point. I mean, it doesn't even have to be expensive for Fred to wreck it, as I look around and spot my papier mâché JUPITER that he squished flat with his bottom.

'Um, I'm not sure how to tell you this.' Dad is standing at the bedroom doorway with a trowel in his hand. 'But Fred's been widdling in the plant pots again. Your pansies have had it.'

'Fred!' Mum cries. 'Why can't you widdle in the toilet like normal people?'

Why indeed.

'Cos of the lav-lav snakes.' Fred twiddles the cotton dangling from his T-shirt.

'There aren't any snakes living in the toilet waiting to bite your bum,' Mum reminds him. 'I don't know where you get these fantastical ideas from, you little monkey-flea.'

And yet it's Mum who tells us that every time we leave the loo seat up a fairy dies.

She goes to walk out of the room, but stops

suddenly at the sound of a disgusting crunch. She's just stepped on a snail. With her bare foot.

> ## ARRRRGGGHHHH!
> **GET THESE SNAILS OUT OF HERE OR MUM WON'T BE RESPONSIBLE FOR HER ACTIONS!**

She always talks in the third person when she's really mad.

My parents don't get my obsession with space at all. I must have discovered it all by myself. Maybe it was when I spotted the moving point of the International Space Station and waved to the astronauts. Or found out the glinting red star of Betelgeuse will one day explode into a supernova. Or when I counted meteors on a cold December night (forty-two if you're asking).

MY GENERAL STATE OF MIND

OVER THE MOON

SUNNY

CALM

OK

PHEW

NOT OK

ALARMED

NEED CAKE

STORMY

BLACK HOLE OF DOOM

But I've got a plan. There's a science fair coming up. A space-themed science fair. And guess what the first prize is? Not crazy golf clubs, that's for sure. It's about time I put Operation Stanley Wins A Telescope (SWAT) into action.

I put on my slippers, not wishing to get squished snail bits on my bare feet, only to discover they're full of toothpaste (again). If I had a book about Fred I would have known that was about to happen, but I've had to survive the hard way.

WELCOME TO MY UNIVERSE.

HELP!!!

⤷ DAY-OUT-WITH-A-BRUV SURVIVAL KIT

'Mummy, why is there a horse following us?'
'That's not a horse, Freddie, it's my flip-flops.'

It's Museum Activity Day—a chance for Mum to dump Fred with me so she can lounge in the cafe.

'I'd like a cappuccino and a chance to gather my thoughts too,' I complain.

It takes about **230 MILLION YEARS** for our solar system to make one full turn around the black hole at the centre of the **MILKY WAY**. Which is about how long it feels when I have to look after Fred.

'Morning boys!' beams Mary, struggling with

OVER THE MOON

SUNNY

CALM

OK

PHEW

NOT OK

ALARMED

NEED CAKE

STORMY

BLACK HOLE OF DOOM

MY GENERAL STATE OF MIND

a mountain of clipboards. 'I've got a brand new quiz for you! Fill it in to get a pencil!'

Believe me, it isn't a brand new quiz—it's the same questions in a different order. And the irony that you have to bring a pencil to fill it in to get a pencil is not lost on me.

At least I've made sure to pack my **DAY-OUT-WITH-A-BRUV SURVIVAL KIT**, something every lumbered older sibling should own, and the number one item of which is **A WATCH.** May sound unremarkable, but you don't want to be looking after them for a minute more than you have to. Mainly because parents and younger bruvs are on completely different time zones:

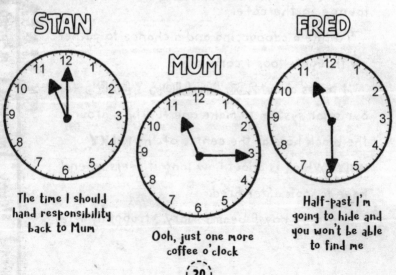

STAN

The time I should hand responsibility back to Mum

MUM

Ooh, just one more coffee o'clock

FRED

Half-past I'm going to hide and you won't be able to find me

'Are you going to help fill in the exciting quiz, Freddie?' Mum asks, but he's already run off into the grand hall clutching his pillow, because he's about to make himself very comfy in front of one particular exhibit.

You'd think a museum was ripe for a five-year-old to destroy, and most of them have a go—banging on the glass cabinets, prodding the glass cabinets, licking the glass cabinets (basically ignoring all the DO NOT BANG, PROD, OR LICK THE GLASS CABINETS signs.)

But Freddie just becomes transfixed. Not by the jewel-coloured beetles, the glow-in-the-dark minerals, or even the stuffed badger (always freaks me out). Fred sits on his pillow in a trance underneath RORY. He only comes to see Rory. Rory is everything to him. Rory holds the power that I wish to hold—to get my brother to sit still for more than five minutes without picking his nose.

Rory would have a job picking HIS nose, mind, because he's a T-rex. Obviously

OVER THE MOON
SUNNY
CALM
OK
PHEW
NOT OK
ALARMED
NEED CAKE
STORMY
BLACK HOLE OF DOOM

MY GENERAL STATE OF MIND

21

not a live one, otherwise
Mum wouldn't allow Freddie
to sit there for hours on end
while she supped cappuccinos.

'Hello Mister Bushy Eyebrows!'

'Oh . . . hello again, Fred.'

I'm amazed Mr Hadfield strays
anywhere near my brother's orbit, knowing the
onslaught of questions he always fires at him.
It must be like being caught in the immense
gravity of JUPITER. Perhaps he's just checking
Freddie isn't sneaking bits of Rory out every time
he visits so he can rebuild him in our bedroom.

'Is he real?' he asks, stretching his neck to look
up at him.

Mr Hadfield has to answer this Every. Single.
Time.

'He is indeed real, and was born during the
upper cretaceous period,' he says, leaning
back and putting his hands in his tweed jacket
pockets. 'A theropod up to twelve metres long,
with teeth the size of bananas, weighing more
than six tonnes, becoming extinct approximately

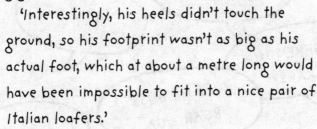

sixty-five million—'

'Did he wear shoes?'
Fred is now comparing his
tiny trainer against Rory's
gigantic feet.

'Interestingly, his heels didn't touch the
ground, so his footprint wasn't as big as his
actual foot, which at about a metre long would
have been impossible to fit into a nice pair of
Italian loafers.'

'Will he come alive at night?'

'No. Remember I told you before—he's a
fossil,' he looks down at Fred through his
half-moon glasses. 'But when he WAS alive,
Rory would have roamed North America
amongst the—'

'I think he <u>DOES</u> come alive at night and
roars all over the place.'

'Well, he really doesn't.'

'But you don't know, cos you're not here.'

'True, young fellow-me-lad, but I'm an
expert at this sort of thing. And also we have
CCTV in every—'

MY GENERAL STATE OF MIND

OVER THE MOON

SUNNY

CALM

OK

PHEW

NOT OK

ALARMED

NEED CAKE

STORMY

BLACK HOLE OF DOOM

'I've . . . just got to go and polish the butterfly cabinet . . . .' Mr Hadfield scarpers, mopping his brow.

He clearly hasn't heard of the number two item in my essential sibling excursion equipment: **NOISE-CANCELLING HEADPHONES**. The only way to guarantee not to hear another question. Which means I can concentrate on writing out my plan for Operation SWAT:

1. Get school to enter competition.
2. Put together fantastic SWAT Team (or anyone in Year Six who says yes).
3. Come up with exciting interactive space-themed experiment (provide cake for distraction if interactive space-themed experiment isn't that exciting).
4. **WIN** (obvs).
5. **THE END**.

   Oh, and

6. Promise Dad you'll go into his painting and decorating business if he'll convert his shed into an observatory (remember to be rubbish at painting and decorating so you can easily get out of promise).

OVER THE MOON

SUNNY

CALM

OK

PHEW

NOT OK

ALARMED

NEED CAKE

STORMY

BLACK HOLE of DOOM

MY GENERAL STATE OF MIND

I've already got an idea for the experiment from my favourite exhibit in the museum. You could easily walk past it, especially as it's right next to the sparkly golden pyrite and glistening quartz. It looks like a splat of dark rock, and feels rough like a piece of metal, with rusty orange flecks and thumbprint-sized dimples. But it's an iron meteorite that fell to EARTH, and is *FOUR AND A HALF BILLION YEARS OLD*. It's as old as the EARTH. From when the solar system began. And amazingly, the museum let you touch it. Although right now someone else has got their mitts all over it.

'Oi! I was here first you landlubber!'

There's a Freddie-sized person staring up at me. A little girl that's more blonde fluffy hair than anything else. Flossie McGregor. Flossie McGregor who thinks she's an actual pirate.

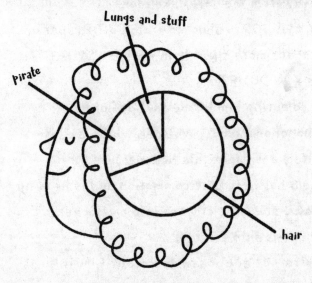

COMPOSITION of FLOSSIE MCGREGOR

Lungs and stuff

pirate

hair

She's not even studying it properly, she's staring into the distance.

'Freddie ahoy,' she whispers, holding her hands up like a telescope in the direction of my brother.

'You're spying on him?'

'You should be spying as well. I don't fink he should be doing that, me hearties.'

I part Flossie's hair to get a closer look. Fred is leant over Rory's feet, looking busy.

Fred looking busy is never a good sign. I

MY GENERAL STATE OF MIND

OVER THE MOON | SUNNY | CALM | OK | PHEW | NOT OK | ALARMED | NEED CAKE | STORMY | BLACK HOLE OF DOOM quickly walk over towards my brother, and pull him away from the T-rex skeleton.

'OH. MY. GOD.' I shout in a kind of whispery shout that's more shout than whisper. 'WHAT HAVE YOU DONE?'

'I'm colouring him in,' he says defiantly.

'Nononononono!' I whisper, which is definitely a whisper this time because Mr Hadfield has heard the commotion and is heading our way. I stuff the crayons into my pocket.

'But all his skin fell off.'

'You're not supposed to colour him in! People expect to see . . . bone-coloured bones, not rainbow-coloured ones!' I pull out the number three item in my **DAY-OUT-WITH-A-BRUV SURVIVAL KIT—WET WIPES**—and start rubbing the bright green and yellow fossils, praying forgiveness to the Dinosaur God and thanking him for water-based crayons.

'Everything all right over here, young fellow-me-lads?'

'Yep!' I squeak, shoving a stray crayon under a nearby cabinet with my foot.

'Need any help?'

'Nope.'

'Sure?'

And then I spot Flossie heading towards us. She's gonna spill the beans. We'll have to pay sixty-five million pounds for a new T-rex skeleton and there'll be no more sweets for six years. My Bruv Pressure is peaking.

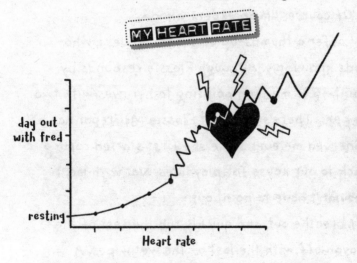

MY HEART RATE

day out
with fred

resting

Heart rate

I pull out the number four item in my **DAY-OUT-WITH-A-BRUV SURVIVAL KIT**: HAT AND SUNGLASSES to avoid recognition should an embarrassing episode occur. Although it may already be too late.

OVER THE MOON

SUNNY

CALM

OK

PHEW

NOT OK

ALARMED

NEED CAKE

STORMY

BLACK HOLE OF DOOM

MY GENERAL STATE OF MIND

'Oi! Mister Bushy Eyebrows!' Flossie tugs at Mr Hadfield's trouser leg, and I put my hands together, pleading for mercy at the hands of a girl with enough hair for six people. 'Stanley let his brother—'

'Excuse me! Can you tell me about the butterfly display, right over there, far away from this T-rex?' It's Jess McGregor, Flossie's older sister.

'Of course, I'm an expert y'know.'

I offer a thumbs-up of thanks to Jess, who nods knowingly. Although Flossie responds by pointing to me then pointing to her eyes with two fingers. There's no doubt Flossie McGregor has unnerved me ever since she first started coming back to our house for playdates. Not with me, I shouldn't have to point out.

I breathe out, and quickly rub the rest of the crayon off with the last of the wet wipes. A packet doesn't last long with a younger bruv in tow—I'm constantly cleaning his mucky finger-prints off dogs, TV screens, and cream cakes.

Mum's now at the exit, looking impatiently at her watch. The chaos has made us late even by her time zone.

'We've got to go, Fred, and thank your lucky stars that crayon's come off.'

But he's flopped down on top of his pillow and folded his arms in a strop.

RECIPE FOR DISASTER

1 Bruv
6 Crayons

Mix in a public place

'Not fanking lucky stars for nuffink. Not going nonewhere cos you shouted.'

'Mum's waiting.' I point towards the arm-flapping evidence. 'How did you even get hold of the crayons anyway?'

'Not telling,' he mimes zipping his eyes. CRAYONS ARE BANNED FROM OUTINGS. He scribbled Rory on a painting at the garden centre cafe last week. Mum had to buy it for fifty-five pounds and demanded Mum o'clock for the rest of the day.

'If you don't tell me,' I put my hand next to Rory's skeleton, 'I'll pull out his leg bone and he'll DIE ALL OVER AGAIN.'

'DON'T! I'll tell you!' and he whispers

OVER THE MOON

SUNNY

CALM

OK

PHEW

NOT OK

ALARMED

NEED CAKE

STORMY

BLACK HOLE of DOOM

MY GENERAL STATE OF MIND

quietly, 'I hidden them in my pillowcase.'

Mum's now going red in the face, though she'd be going purple if she knew what was really going on.

'Time to go, NOW,' I plead, holding out my hand.

'Make me.'

I'm determined not to drag him along the floor by his arms again. It's time for the lure. Time for the final item in my **DAY-OUT-WITH-A-BRUV SURVIVAL KIT:**

CAKE-ON-A-STICK

Cake is power. I know they say knowledge is power, but it isn't. It's cake.

Especially if it's on a stick.

↳ TRICKS-UP-YOUR-SLEEVE

'It's taking me seven whole years to do this homework!' moans Fred.

He's only five.

'Stan, help him out would you?' Mum says.

I've tried to get out of doing my brother's homework before by joining the after school club. But unfortunately I'm not a natural at country dancing, so I fetch my felt tips.

'I've got to draw a stupid healthy meal, with scusting vegetables and everything,' Fred says holding up a paper plate. 'Not even no pudding.'

'Just doodle some green squiggles on it,' I suggest. 'And call it broccoli.'

But instead he picks up a brown felt-tip and

dots the plate in Chocco Pops so furiously that the end of the pen gets wedged inside and yet he still keeps going.

'Fred,' I tut. 'Chocolate isn't one of your five-a-day.'

'Yes it is!' he shouts, standing on his chair and spilling the remnants of his juice all over my carefully drawn solar system homework.

'At least they kind of look like stars,' Mum says, pointing to the flecks of sticky orange strewn throughout the Kuiper Belt. 'Go hang your homework on the washing line, love. It's tea time.'

Family tea. Another hazard in the home where you not only need your wits about you, but some **Tricks-Up-Your-Sleeve**, and if you can get away with it, some biscuits up your sleeve too.

Before sitting down, arm yourself with the following:

o BLU TACK

o WATERPROOF TROUSERS

o BISCUITS UP YOUR SLEEVES

The whole family in a confined space around the kitchen table is a situation waiting to blow. And usually over what gets served up.

This is where cake comes in handy again. Cake can help explain a multitude of things. You may call it a pie chart, but I call it a cake chart.

Who would choose pie over cake?

Not me.

HERE ARE TWO CAKE CHARTS ABOUT **CAKE**

TYPES OF CAKE

BEETROOT CAKE
1%

99%
YUMMY CAKE

TYPES OF CAKE MY MUM BAKES

BEETROOT CAKE
100%

OVER THE MOON
SUNNY
CALM
OK
PHEW
NOT OK
ALARMED
NEED CAKE
STORMY
BLACK HOLE OF DOOM

MY GENERAL STATE OF MIND

'It's the only way I can get Fred to eat vegetables,' shrugs Mum.

Fred's favourite dinner is 'crisps and rice' and I'm not even joking. Most of my dinners revolve around what he will and won't eat. Never mind what I want to eat (a roast dinner that doesn't involve Pringles and egg fried rice if you're asking).

Mum's obviously feeling brave today by putting something new on the table: spaghetti Bolognese.

'I spy with my little eye . . . somefing beginning with scuh . . .' Freddie grumbles. 'Scusting!'

'Life's a journey, not a bus stop,' Mum says. 'So hop on the Bolognese bus before we drive off to destination pudding without you.'

'I can't fit any more food in my tummy,' Fred moans, lifting his top and shoving out his belly.

'You haven't eaten any food yet, sunshine,' Dad lowers his newspaper.

'I ate nine Jammy Dodgers after school,' and then he gasps and covers his mouth.

'I hid that biscuit barrel on top of the cupboard you crafty fox!' Mum exclaims.

OVER THE MOON

SUNNY

CALM

OK

PHEW

NOT OK

ALARMED

NEED CAKE

STORMY

BLACK HOLE of DOOM

MY GENERAL STATE OF MIND

TROUBLESHOOTING BISCUITS

Store your biscuit stash in hollowed-out books (don't hollow out your own books—sacrilege!—I've hollowed out Dad's unread football manager biographies that are stacked at the back of the cupboard).

Fred sniffs out biscuits like a pig sniffs out whatever pigs sniff out. Give him any house, in any town, in any country, and he'll find them, even if there's a national biscuit shortage.

'Just put brown sauce on it, Fred,' Dad says, squeezing it all over his spaghetti.

'You don't need sauce on the authentic flavours of Italy!' Mum cries.

'It's not Italy, it's yuck!' Fred pushes his plate so far across the table, it ALMOST knocks my cup over, but I remembered to stick it down with **BLU TACK**.

'Ooh, have you seen this?' Dad folds his newspaper back and turns it around. 'Look who's in the paper.'

Freddie's eyes pop open as he leans forward to get a better look, putting his elbow in my dinner.

'RORY!' he yells.

'Get your arm out of my Bolognese!' I yell back.

He points, as though that makes up for it. It IS Rory, I'll give him that. Along with the large headline:

DINO TO GO

Although I'm more taken by the science fair entry form on the other page and make a mental note to cut it out.

'Let me see.' Freddie climbs forward even more and puts his knee in my spaghetti.

'Mum! Tell Fred to get out of my dinner!'

'Why's Rory in the paper? Is he coming back to life?'

'No he's not, Fred,' Dad replies, half reading the article. 'It says they're replacing Rory with an exhibition relevant to today's pressing issues. What? How to get rid of slugs?'

Fred looks angry-puzzled, as he always does when he doesn't understand something. Like the time I told him he couldn't keep ringing Gran, burping, and putting the phone down.

'They're getting rid of Rory?' Mum says, twirling her spaghetti. 'Gosh. He was even there when I was little.'

'No more Rory?' Freddie frowns heavily.

'I'm sure the new exhibition will be awesome,' I try to say cheerfully. 'There might even be new questions.'

'Nonebody talk to me!' He flips his plate of spaghetti up in the air and on to my lap, then rushes upstairs to our bedroom.

'Oi!' yells Dad. 'I could have eaten that!'

The classic plate flip. Luckily I'm wearing WATERPROOF TROUSERS—there's nothing worse than sitting in a pair of spaghetti-soaked jeans. Apart from overheating in spaghetti-soaked waterproof trousers.

MY GENERAL STATE OF MIND

OVER THE MOON

SUNNY

CALM

OK

PHEW

NOT OK

ALARMED

NEED CAKE

STORMY

BLACK HOLE OF DOOM

'Why can't we have just one teatime that doesn't descend into chaos?' moans Mum. 'Stan, go and have a word with your brother.'

'But I'm trying to eat . . .' I look at the squashed mess on my plate, with bits of grass from Fred's grass-stained knees, mud from his mud-stained elbows, and some other green bits I don't want to study too closely. *CAN I GET A BOGEY WITH MY BOLOGNESE?* said no one ever.

Quite often you won't get to finish your tea and this is where **BISCUITS UP YOUR SLEEVES** come in handy to stave off the hunger. Remember—the bigger the jumper, the more biscuits you can stuff up the sleeves.

I reluctantly climb the stairs to find Fred lying on MY bed, having wiped his Bolognese limbs on MY pillow, sobbing snotty tears all over MY pyjamas. Stupid me. I forgot to laminate my whole bed.

'Listen, it'll be fine, Fred, you'll see,' I try to convince

TAKE ACTION!

Swap your Bolognese-destroyed pillow with Dad's

him, reading aloud from the paper. 'There's going to be a GIANT MODEL EARTH EXPLORING THE EFFECTS OF CLIMATE CHANGE.'

'Don't care.'

'Which is precisely why we need this exhibition! It's up to your generation to SAVE THE PLANET by ... um ... BUILDING A NEWLY EXPANDED COFFEE SHOP WITH DELICIOUS PASTRIES.'

'Do I like 'licious pastries?' he sniffs, lifting his head.

'It's basically flat cake, so yes,' I go to rub his hair affectionately but remember it smells of wet donkey.

'I want Rory ...' he looks about to burst into tears again—dangerously near my drawing of a solar eclipse in pastels which I've carelessly left on my bedside table instead of ON TOP OF THE WARDROBE OUT OF REACH.

'I'll run you a bath ... biggest bubbles on the planet ...' I manage to tempt him away from my masterpiece.

OVER THE MOON
SUNNY
CALM
OK
PHEW
NOT OK
ALARMED
NEED CAKE
STORMY
BLACK HOLE OF DOOM

MY GENERAL STATE OF MIND

Only Fred decides to make an indoor ocean by splashing water all over the bathroom floor.

'You really should know better than to let him near taps,' Mum sighs. 'You'll have to read his bedtime story while I mop it up.'

'Oh but—'

'Buts are for pants! Mum can't do everything round here, believe me Mum feels like she does everything round here, but it's already half-past Mum o'clock!'

Fair enough.

'What about Dad?'

'I'm cleaning the mess in the kitchen!' Dad yells up, clearly with a mouthful of food. 'It's going to take me a good twenty-minutes-to-half-an-hour to eat all this spaghetti.'

Precisely the time it takes to read Fred's favourite book—Two by Two. It's only eight pages, but he insists on naming every pair of animals lining up to go inside Noah's Ark. And even though I've read it to him 3,581 times, he

RECIPE FOR DISASTER
* 1 Bruv
* 80 Litres of water
* Mix to make an indoor ocean

always gets the animals wrong.

At least there's no trace of nose debris on his face after the flood. He smells of coconut as he snuggles up beside me, shoving his cold feet under mine inside my slippers.

'Noah has built a wooden ark to sail away to safety. Let's see what animals are coming aboard today . . .' I flip the page.

'Malingos?' Freddie interrupts.

'No.'

MINGOS? PONGOS?

IT'S AN OSTRICH

One page later and it happens all over again.

ARMALLILOS?

MARMALLILOS?

CROCADILLOS?

43

'Look, it's quite clearly a meerkat.'

Cut to me squillions of years later and I'm a skeleton surrounded by dust and tarantulas, people are living on MARS, and Fred's still only on page two. Perhaps we should take up Gran's suggestion and take him to the zoo.

Then he stops, and pulls a face so crumpled, I can't see his eyes.

'Why didn't Mr Noah put the T-rexes on his ark?'

'Do you ever listen to a word I say?'

'Nope.'

'Sixty-five million years ago an enormous meteorite crashed to Earth,' I recite. 'It filled the air with so much dust it blocked out the sun. The plants died, then the plant-eaters died, then the meat-eaters died—'

'Then the pudding-eaters died?'

'Something like that. But it wiped out all the dinosaurs, Fred.'

He looks at me for a moment, as though he truly understands the enormity of what I've just told him, the real reason why Rory stands in a museum without his skin. But no.

'He should have eaten crisps and rice,' and he starts jumping up and down on my bed.

'Right. Sleepy times,' I say, lifting him off and handing back the dinosaur toys he brought with him. 'You really should get Mum to wash them, they're covered in dust—'

AAAAAA-CHOOOOOO!

he sneezes all over my bedside table. All over my interpretation of a solar eclipse in pastels. Which now has six more solar flares than it did before. Of all the tricks I keep up my sleeve, why isn't one of them a tissue?

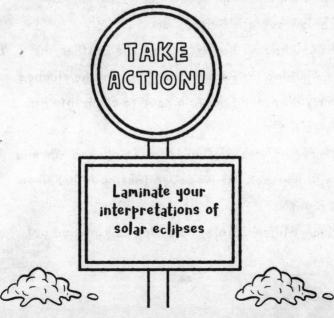

TAKE ACTION!

Laminate your interpretations of solar eclipses

⮕ SURVIVING SCHOOL

Sirius is the brightest star in our night sky. It's 8.6 light years away, and often mistaken for a UFO because it twinkles different colours. None of these things could describe my best mate Liam. But Sirius does have a small white dwarf companion, and Liam never lets me forget how far below average height I am.

'As you know I haven't got a little brother,' he says, flicking his hair. 'But if I did, and he climbed into my dinner, I'd deffolo have to climb into his. Only fair.'

'You've no idea. Nothing comes between him and Rory,' I whisper. 'He was even roaring in his sleep last night.'

'Liam Miller! Stanley Fox! Stop talking and get

on with your Venn diagrams!' Mr Fisher yells.

Maths on a Monday morning should be made illegal. However, I like the idea of a Venn diagram as a new way of displaying data, and go a bit off topic.

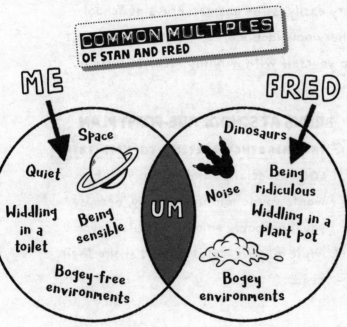

COMMON MULTIPLES
OF STAN AND FRED

ME

FRED

Space

Quiet

Dinosaurs

Being ridiculous

Widdling in a toilet

Being sensible

Noise

UM

Widdling in a plant pot

Bogey-free environments

Bogey environments

'Bogey environments?' Mr Fisher bellows over my shoulder. 'Tell me, Mr Fox, I appear to have forgotten, is that a common multiple of three and five?'

'Gulp. Dunno.'

OVER THE MOON

SUNNY

CALM

OK

PHEW

NOT OK

ALARMED

NEED CAKE

STORMY

BLACK HOLE OF DOOM

MY GENERAL STATE OF MIND

And yes, I did say gulp out loud. Worse still, illegal maths has got me staying in at break with a reflection sheet and a load of Venn diagrams to complete. How come my brother gets me into trouble even when he's not around?

Very easily is the answer. Bruvs at School—another unavoidable area of life, so you'd best equip yourself with winning ideas to survive.

BRUVS AT SCHOOL FIVE-POINT PLAN

- **THE EMERGENCY PRETEND-TO-NEED-THE-LOO-** especially handy when your bruv wants you to join in skipping, because you'll probably enjoy it a bit too much while all your mates tut and shake their heads.

- **THE FIRST AID ROOM-** this will become one of your best allies, particularly when you need a lie-down because he decided to show-and-tell a photo of you on the potty in the 'Meet-My-Family Assembly'.

* **THE SPARE JUMPER** - invaluable for the school photo as he's always covered in what you hope is mud, and Mum will blame you if you don't clean him up.

* **THE STOPWATCH** - not only so you can fairly divide your breaktime between your mates and your younger bruv (80:20 obvs), but so you know exactly when to step in and rescue him from the monkey bars before his arms fall off.

* **THE '1001 SPACE FACTS' BOOK** - so when Mum's hauled in to see the teacher at the end of the day to 'have a quick word about Fred, Mrs Fox', you've got something to do because it usually means an hour-long meeting with the head teacher, the dinner lady, and a pot plant containing the leftovers of Fred's lunch.

Oh. And try not to go off topic in maths.

MY GENERAL STATE OF MIND

OVER THE MOON
SUNNY
CALM
OK
PHEW
NOT OK
ALARMED
NEED CAKE
STORMY
BLACK HOLE OF DOOM

While I'm writing out how to improve my behaviour by not making up Venn diagrams, I get interrupted by Mrs Parker, the Reception Class teacher.

'Sorry to barge in.' She looks over at the teaching assistant who's supervising. 'I need to borrow Stanley for a moment.'

Fred's stood in the corridor covered in snot and tears.

'Blimey, what happened to you?' I exclaim.

'He says Rory's disappeared . . . is that a new situation at home we should be aware of?' Mrs Parker does her best concerned face.

'Eh?'

'Is Rory a family member, or a pet perhaps?'

'Oh no . . . he's a T-rex.'

'I see . . . um, actually I don't.'

I explain to her about the newspaper article.

'They're getting rid of the T-rex? Really? But he's been there for ever . . .'

Which sets him off all over again.

'Freddie, it's OK.' Mrs Parker tries to dab him with a tissue from a safe distance. 'I'm sure the museum will have something equally magnificent for you to go and visit.'

'No they won't!' he blubs. 'Except for 'licious pastries . . .'

'Look, come and sit with your brother for the rest of break and calm down.'

While Fred leans on my arm, stutter sobbing, I pull out the science fair entry form. Mrs Parker's always encouraged my love of space. Ever since I first joined Camford Primary and she showed us how a SOLAR ECLIPSE works. Most of the other kids wanted to eat the orange that represented the sun, but me? I wanted to know more about the orange. By which I mean the sun, obviously. I already knew all I needed to know about oranges.

'There's a chance to win a telescope, miss.'

MY GENERAL STATE OF MIND

OVER THE MOON
SUNNY
CALM
OK
PHEW
NOT OK
ALARMED
NEED CAKE
STORMY
BLACK HOLE OF DOOM

'I'll chat to the head, Stanley, leave it with me.' She waves it in the air while walking out of the door. 'Mrs Riley won't easily pass up an opportunity to beat Larkfield Primary, that's for sure.'

Just like Fred won't easily pass up an opportunity to scribble a dinosaur all over my Venn diagrams.

'Fred! What have you done?'

His bottom lip wobbles and he starts sobbing again. I bring him in for the **SACRIFICE HUG**: sacrificing my jumper for everything on his face.

'Right, get back to class, the bell's gone.' I gradually unlock his tight grip around my neck. 'See you at lunchtime.'

I sigh at my ruined schoolwork, as does Mr Fisher who's just walked into the classroom.

'Looks like you've got homework, Mr Fox.'

'Yes, Mr Fisher. Promise I'll get it finished. Minus the dinosaur.'

Although I haven't got high hopes. It's quite impossible to hand in homework unscathed when there's a Fred around, as my JUICE-FLECKED SOLAR SYSTEM DRAWING would agree. So arm yourself with some excuses (maybe not these ones):

TURN SIDEWAYS FOR MY AMAZING GRAPH

HOMEWORK EXCUSES

PUNISHMENT

- reflection sheet
- made to do again
- litter-picking duty
- luckily I got away with it

- It's currently stuck to the kitchen floor
- My brother sat on it
- It should be dry by thursday
- I don't know
- Fred thought it could use some ketchup
- Well at least it made a nice paper aeroplane

MARS is known as the red planet because it's covered in a fine dust of iron oxide. It's basically rusty. Which is what Mrs Gravy's face always looks like when she's been cooking all morning.

'I got me special veg curry today, followed by pear crumble,' she says, slopping it on to my tray. 'D'you want gravy with that?'

This is why we call her Mrs Gravy. She even puts it on fish fingers.

'Not today thanks,' but I'm too slow and a great splodge of thick-skinned meat tar lands on my pudding. Still, it makes a change from crisps and rice.

At that moment Flossie McGregor walks past, snarling: 'Beware the black spot, yer scurvy dog.'

'Wos that all about?' Liam frowns.

'I dunno . . . but doesn't the black spot mean imminent death?'

'You don't wanna mess with Flossie—she's not only got an older sister, she's got an older brother. We're talking teenager. Tall one. With biceps.'

Fred runs over with his food tray and tips his leftovers on to mine.

'Leave it out, bruv!'

'I've told you before,' he whinges, 'I'm not eating broccoli at all.'

'I don't want it either, although I'm not sure it is broccoli. Put it in the food waste.'

'Don't make me ... Mrs Gravy stares all madly and I get shaky legs.'

Can't blame him for that. She does tend to stare daggers at anyone who doesn't eat her food. Which she does to me when I scrape Fred's regurgitated broccoli in the bin.

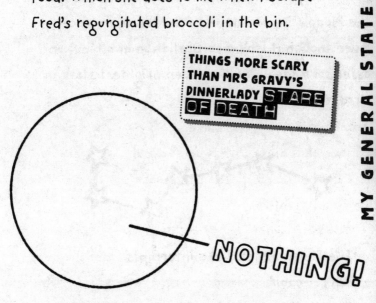

THINGS MORE SCARY THAN MRS GRAVY'S DINNERLADY STARE OF DEATH

NOTHING!

'Game of zombie tag?' Liam suggests as we head out for break.

'Can't. Gotta check something out.'

'But we had plans. Special plans. <u>SPLANS</u>.'

'Splans will have to wait.'

Jess McGregor is sat on the bench reading a book.

'Yo!' I shout, and wonder why, seeing as it's the kind of thing Dad says.

'Hi Stan.' She barely looks up and I notice she's studying a book about constellations.

'What's your favourite? I mean, everyone says the Plough,' I point to the freckles on my face, 'even though it isn't a constellation at all, but an asterism made up of the seven brightest stars in Ursa Major—'

'The Seven Sisters,' she interrupts.

'Oh . . . cool.'

'Sometimes I only see it as a fuzzy blob—but when you look through binoculars, you realize there's more than meets the eye. So although you don't notice it straight away, it's there, and deserves to be noticed.'

'Um, yeah, definitely. Anyway, just wanted to say thanks for the other day, y'know, not grassing us up to Mr Hadfield.'

'That's fine. I know the score.'

'And, um, I wondered if you knew what's wrong with Flossie?'

'What's RIGHT with Flossie?' she looks up and over to where her younger sister is 'organizing' her crewmates on the climbing frame.

'I don't think she likes me,' I shrug.

'Do you want her to like you?'

'Um, well, I'm not THAT bothered. Just she can be a bit . . .'

'Piratey?' Jess stands up and walks over to her. 'Flossie! We need a parley!'

'I'm too busy looting!' Flossie shouts, pretending to steer her ship.

'Cool it on the pirate captain thing. You're scaring Stan.'

'Ha, ha, you're not scaring me!' I laugh

OVER THE MOON

SUNNY

CALM

OK

PHEW

NOT OK

ALARMED

NEED CAKE

STORMY

BLACK HOLE of DOOM

MY GENERAL STATE OF MIND

nervously from behind Jess's shoulder. 'Just wondered why you keep doing the eye thing, like you're sort of watching me.'

'Cos I'm wotching you, yer mangly scallywag.'

'Oh. That's all right then. I mean, that isn't all right then . . . what have I done to deserve—'

'I can't hear you—I'm in the Caribbean.' Flossie pouts, her hair blowing in the breeze. 'Prime the crew Mr Smee! Sea beasties ahead!'

'Just be thankful you're not Mr Smee,' Jess shrugs, pointing to Maisy Watlington from Year One. 'She's had to walk the plank three times this week. AND IT'S ONLY MONDAY.'

⮑ THE FIVE LEVELS OF HUMILIATION

The reason why gold is so rare, is that it's forged in the last seconds of a dying star's life—A SUPERNOVA EXPLOSION. I think that's where Grans are made too.

Due to the lack of yummy cake at home, I get my cake fix elsewhere:

MY GENERAL STATE OF MIND

OVER THE MOON
SUNNY
CALM
OK
PHEW
NOT OK
ALARMED
NEED CAKE
STORMY
BLACK HOLE of DOOM

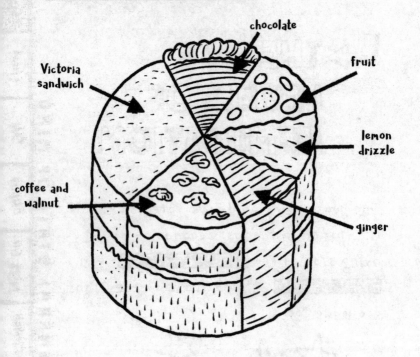

And that was just LAST WEDNESDAY.

She's always baking cakes for fundraisers, neighbours, and her tattooist. If there was an international cake competition, Gran would absolutely nail it. She'd absolutely nail a nail too, because she's pretty handy with a hammer. Don't ever make the mistake of calling her over-the-hill, like Dad once did.

'I'M NOT OVER THE HILL. I'M STILL ON THE HILL, WITH A FRUIT-BASED COCKTAIL AND A SALSA INSTRUCTOR CALLED TONY.'

The planet with the most moons is JUPITER. Over sixty at the last count and they're still finding more. I don't think Gran's found any new siblings lately, but she does come from a large family, which means she's got lots of advice on dealing with younger relatives that tend to orbit you all day long.

Gran's already managed to cheer up Fred by letting him jump on her sofa for half an hour.

'Now, I've got a salsa lesson at six o'clock, so look lively, and let's have the latest Fred dramas,' she says, backcombing her spiky blue hair.

'How can I stop Fred putting cheese in my bed?'

'Tell him to grab some crackers too and have a midnight feast.'

I roll my eyes.

'Or you could batten down your duv

OVER THE MOON

SUNNY

CALM

OK

PHEW

NOT OK

ALARMED

NEED CAKE

MY GENERAL STATE OF MIND

luggage straps,' she says, threading rings on all her fingers.

'What will prevent Fred from cutting holes in my T-shirts?'

'That's called punk, Stanley.'

'It's called more hole than T-shirt, Gran.'

'Well, just keep scissors at twice his height with a bit extra for luck.'

'Is there a way to thwart Fred's attempts to fart in my school bag every day?'

'You could fart in his too.'

'Gran, that's disgusting.'

'Padlock anything with a zip. But you could try fun sometimes, Stan. Never know, you might just enjoy yourself.' She unclicks her lipstick and smudges it over her mouth.

'There's nothing fun about Fred wiping his snot on my shoulders. How can I stop it happening? Apart from laminating my jumper.'

'What you need is a tea towel. There's only so many times you can put up with debris on your leather jacket, know what I mean?' she says, shrugging hers on and turning up the collar. 'You'll never catch me in a cardigan—that way leads the path to Michael Ball and pop socks.'

'Um . . . you were saying about tea towels?'

'Sling one over your shoulder. Trust me—it'll mop up snot, dribble, and fruit-based cocktails. Plus you'll be able to instantly help out with the washing-up. Two-for-one.'

Gran's brilliant at advice. Although Mum often complains, 'She knows nothing of modern parenting, Stanley, it takes more than cake to bring up a family.'

UM, NO IT DOESN'T, I always reply in my head so she can't send me to my room.

My thoughts are interrupted by Gran's jangling necklaces as she salsas round the kitchen: 'Remember, Stanley, get through life with a skip in your step, and never turn down cake!'

'I'm good at the cake bit!' I mumble through mouthfuls of buttercream.

Liam is horrified at my tea-towel epaulettes

MY GENERAL STATE OF MIND

OVER THE MOON

SUNNY

CALM

OK

PHEW

NOT OK

ALARMED

NEED CAKE

STORMY

BLACK HOLE of DOOM

in register next morning, especially as they don't exactly match my red jumper. One has white and green checks. The other has pigs on.

'You're a fashion disastrophe, bro,' he tuts. 'Surely the easiest thing to do is wear several jumpers at once and remove one each time you have a snot-based incident.'

'I did think of that. But you've got your basic overheating issue.'

Unfortunately I failed to overlook the basic 'THAT DOESN'T LOOK MUCH LIKE SCHOOL UNIFORM TO ME, STANLEY FOX' issue. My shoulder accessories get me staying in for most of lunch with a reflection sheet (NOTE TO SELF: SNOT SHOULDERS STILL TO BE RESOLVED).

While I'm writing out the correct items of Camford Primary School's uniform (definitely NOT the eyepatch I saw Flossie McGregor wearing this morning), I get interrupted by Mrs Parker. Again.

'Sorry to barge in,' she looks over at the teaching assistant. 'I need to chat to Stanley.'

'What's Fred done this time?' I sigh.

'Nothing. Oh, that's not quite true, but it's for

your mother to deal with later. I spoke to Mrs Riley about the science fair. Get yourself a team of four by Monday and we're on the way to that telescope.'

'Thanks, miss!'

'It will be SCHOOL property, Stanley, you do realize that don't you?'

'Oh. Yeah. Course.'

That bit wasn't part of <u>OPERATION</u> SWAT. It's STANLEY Wins A Telescope. Not Stanley Wins a Telescope and Gives It To The School (SWATAGITTS).

'But we could start up an **ASTRONOMY CLUB**— and you can look after it some weekends.'

I almost forget to finish my reflection sheet, I've got such a big grin on my face. The prospect of an astronomy club, plus a telescope at weekends, and planning a space-themed project is a dream come true.

And it brings me on to the important subject of **ME-TIME**. This will help keep your mood predominantly sunny, giving you the armour to deal with small-year-olds. Time spent

doing your favourite activity will just about keep
you sane when you discover upon going to the
bathroom that your favourite socks have soaked
up a puddle of bruv widdle.

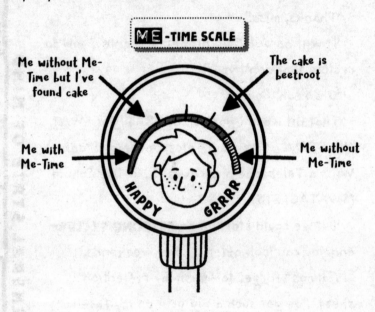

ME-TIME SCALE

Me without Me-
Time but I've
found cake

The cake is
beetroot

Me with
Me-Time

Me without
Me-Time

HAPPY   GRRRR

I catch up with Liam and Idris in the playground.
Which I'm not supposed to call the playground
anymore; it's the 'HANGING-OUT SPACE,
DUDE-BRO. WHAT ARE YOU? SOME KIND OF
LUNIAC?'

'Would you rather have a billion pounds and no
brain, or 50p and be a genius?' asks Idris.

There are two things Idris likes doing. One is playing Would You Rather on a daily basis, and the other is computer games. He plays so many, he constantly tries to right-click everything in real life.

'Billion pounds and no brain,' answers Liam.

'Well you're halfway there,' Idris says and Liam nods in agreement.

'I've got one!' I announce. 'Would you rather spend next week being complete and utter dullards, or help out your really brilliant mate with his science fair project?'

'Complete and utter dullards,' they both say together.

'Thanks. That's the last time I help either of you. Don't come knocking on my door when . . . um . . . you need any of the things that only I can do.'

'Yeah, well I'll give you a call if I need a pie chart, Graph Vader,' Liam rolls his eyes.

I spend the rest of break trying to recruit members for my **OPERATION SWAT** Team.

'SORRY BUT I'M ALLERGIC TO SCIENCE';

OVER THE MOON

SUNNY

CALM

OK

PHEW

NOT OK

ALARMED

NEED CAKE

STORMY

BLACK HOLE OF DOOM

MY GENERAL STATE OF MIND

'NO, COS ALL OF A SUDDEN I'VE GOT YAWNING PRACTICE'; 'ARE YOU HAVING A LAUGH?' are some of the really rather rude answers I receive. As well as disappointing Barney Campbell in Year Five who thought he was signing up for dangerous police training.

After lunch we shuffle into the hall for an assembly by Reception Class. I dread these—mostly because Fred likes to share things that really shouldn't be shared. Like the photo of me on the potty. And the time he told everyone 'MY BROTHER'S GOT DIMPLES ON HIS CHEEKS'. Luckily everyone thought he meant my face.

'Hello, children. As it's INTERNATIONAL WISH DAY, Reception Class would like to share their wishes with you,' Mrs Parker announces.

'I didn't even know there was one of them,' Liam whispers.

'I remember it being INTERNATIONAL QUIET DAY on three occasions in the same WEEK when we were in Reception.'

'Thank you Mrs Parker, I can't wait to find out what they are,' says Mrs Riley the head teacher,

who starts to walk along the line. 'So . . .
what's your wish, Amber?'

'To eat all the doughnuts in the world, miss.'

'Lovely. And Flossie, how about you?'

'I wish to sail the seven seas as a cut-throat
pirate, don't need nuffink more than that.'

No surprises there.

Mrs Riley continues, choosing my brother
because he's picking his nose: 'Freddie? Where
do fingers belong?'

'Inside packets of crisps, miss?'

'I think you'll find the answer is *NOT IN
NOSES*. So what's your wish?'

'The thing I really wish for in my life,'
he shouts, with absolutely no need of a
microphone. 'Is to be a genie—'

'Ooh, so you can grant wishes too?' Mrs Riley
questions.

'No,' he looks angry-puzzled. 'So I can be
cleverer and save Rory.'

He means genius. Although the idea of him
being stuck inside an old lamp and shoved at
the back of a cave is quite appealing.

OVER THE MOON

SUNNY

CALM

OK

PHEW

NOT OK

ALARMED

NEED CAKE

STORMY

BLACK HOLE OF DOOM

MY GENERAL STATE OF MIND

'Can I have a wish for my ginormous bruvver now?'

'Oh, how kind, Fred,' Mrs Riley smiles looking over at me. 'Go on then.'

I immediately don't like the sound of this.

'I wish Stanley could have a girlfriend so he's not grumpy. Someone like Jess Mageggor over there,' and he even points.

OH. MY. ACTUAL. GOD.

I sink as far down into the floor as I possibly can (which isn't far because it's a floor), and wish my brother really was stuck at the back of a cave inside a lamp.

'Let's just leave it there shall we?' Mrs Riley talks loudly to cover up the laughter, but nothing can cover up my boiling face which could power all the electricity in the world for a good two years.

There are different levels of humiliation—this one is a **LEVEL FIVE**: THREAT TO HUMANITY.

THEEEE most embarrassing thing that's ever happened to me. Even worse than the time I dressed up as Gandalf for <u>WORLD BOOK DAY</u>, only Mum got the date wrong and I ended up star-jumping in a grey sheet and false beard all through PE. And, unbelievably, even worse than the Level Four I once experienced on a picnic at the park for my birthday, in front of everyone I know and quite a lot I didn't.

'Phewwie!' Liam whistles as we file out of the hall. 'Am I glad *I* don't have a younger bruv!'

'I won't have one either by the time I've finished with him,' I say through gritted teeth, whilst placing my face on the classroom wall to try and take some of the heat out of my cheeks.

MY GENERAL STATE OF MIND

OVER THE MOON
SUNNY
CALM
OK
PHEW
NOT OK
ALARMED
NEED CAKE
STORMY
BLACK HOLE OF DOOM

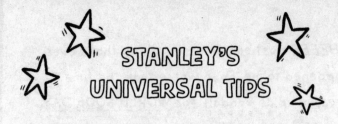

STANLEY'S UNIVERSAL TIPS

HOW TO DEAL WITH THE EMBARRASSMENT CAUSED BY YOUR YOUNGER BROTHER

Don't have a younger brother. Fred has now managed to embarrass me on all five levels of humiliation. And if you don't know what they are, here's a handy guide (including **the picnic at the park incident**):

THE FIVE LEVELS OF HUMILIATION

LEVEL ONE:
MINOR BASHFULNESS
CHEEK COLOUR: dusky pink nebula.

EXAMPLE: Fred telling everyone at a family gathering that he loved me 'ALL THE WAY TO THE RADIATOR AND BACK'.

LEVEL TWO:
MIDDLING SHAME
CHEEK COLOUR: a flushed Mars, rusty red.
EXAMPLE: Fred telling my mates 'WE'VE BEEN PLAYING PRINCESSES LOCKED IN TOWERS ALL WEEKEND!'

LEVEL FIVE: THREAT TO HUMANITY

CHEEK COLOUR: the centre of the sun's core which is thirty million degrees, we're talking flaming Armageddon. Put it this way, you would rather the sun turned into a red giant and swallowed Earth, sacrificing all life on the planet, than endure any more of the distressing embarrassment you're going through.

EXAMPLE: basically anything involving girls + mentions of love, in assembly, in front of the whole school.

LEVEL FOUR: INTRINSIC MORTIFIED DISASTER

CHEEK COLOUR: the surface temperature of Venus, hot enough to melt lead.

EXAMPLE: an extended-family picnic at the park, with cousins I'd never even met before, where there happened to be only lame baby swings. Lame baby swings that Fred encouraged me to have a go on. Only I couldn't get back out. It took a whole hour to release my wedged legs, being stretched and pulled, and eventually dangled upside down by the heftier members of the family so that gravity took over. Unfortunately when I fell out my trousers didn't. And yes, I was wearing space rocket pants.

LEVEL THREE: FLUSTERED DISTRESS

CHEEK COLOUR: the anti-cyclonic storm of Jupiter's Great Red Spot.

EXAMPLE: anything to do with Wee Willie Winkie.

ROOM DIVISION

Because of its slow rotation, **VENUS'S** day is longer than its year. The day I've just had definitely felt like 243 years.

If you did a cross section of a younger bruv's brain, you'd discover the complete lack of embarrassment—it doesn't even exist for them at this age. It's impossible for them to feel it (clearly, if they think just wearing pants everywhere is acceptable), and that is why they can dish it out so easily.

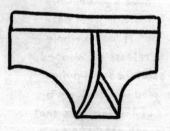

TURN SIDEWAYS FOR MY AMAZING DIAGRAM

CROSS SECTION OF YOUNGER BRUV BRAIN

BLAME FRONTAL LOBE
Who else but me can take responsibility for this?

ANNOYING HEMISPHERE
At its peak around four in the morning

COOKIE HIPPOCAMPUS
Memory of where all the biscuits are stored in the world

CRAYON CORTEX
Are those crayons and can I destroy things with them?

DINOSAUR VISUAL CORTEX
Forges strong attachment to a pile of cretaceous bones

TINY DANGER GLAND
Because I'm invincible

FOOD SENSORY
Reject if healthy

MANIPULATIVE CEREBELLUM
Make parents do exactly what I want

BOGEY NUCLEUS
Honestly, bogies really are food

CORE OF PERFECTLY RATIONAL FEARS
Lav-lav snakes live in the toilet, and great white sharks live under beds

GOOD MANNERS CHASM
Hey, not everyone uses their brain to full capacity

'Mum, you're not gonna believe what Fred said out loud in assembly in front of the WHOLE school this afternoon.' I slump my rucksack down on the living room carpet.

'Ssh, I'm watching the local news,' she interrupts turning up the volume.

'There has been a local outcry over Camford Museum's decision to replace their T-rex with a model Earth. The museum states it's a reflection of today's concerns, however some residents say Rory the T-rex is part of the museum's history, not just our prehistory. This report from Shaznay O'Neil . . .'

'Rory's on the telly!' yells Fred.

'He's sixty-five million years old but is it time for Rory to retire? No, says local resident Jim Noke . . .'
'It's a disgrace, retiring Rory at his age—dinosaurs are an integral part of our planet's past and shouldn't be wiped out like they were sixty-five million years ago. I shall be protesting outside the museum this weekend with a petition, so bring your Save Rory posters!'

MY GENERAL STATE OF MIND

OVER THE MOON

SUNNY

CALM

OK

PHEW

NOT OK

ALARMED

NEED CAKE

STORMY

BLACK HOLE OF DOOM

'But museum director John Banner insists this is the right step forward . . .'

'It's time for Rory to hang up his prehistoric bones and make way for an amazing interactive exhibition that will challenge young minds to think about their responsibility towards Earth. We firmly believe it is a necessary change. A change for the future. Our planet's future. Not its past. But looking forwards in a forward-looking way towards the future.'

'Stinky future!'

Fred stamps his feet, drowning out the rest of the report, and stomps upstairs.

'Anyway, Mum, as I was saying, it was a Level Five humili—'

'I know, Stan, your brother filled me in. And he wasn't being malicious. I mean, Jess McGregor's a nice girl. So chill out poodle feathers.'

'Chill out?'

'Besides, your brother's very anxious at the

moment. I got a phone call from Mrs Parker today. Apparently he's answering Rory to every single question. How many sides does a triangle have? Rory. What colour is the bus? Rory. Can you stop wiping your bogies on the whiteboard? Rory. I'm worried about him . . .'

'I'm worried about ME! Look Mum, I was soooo embarrassed, I wanted Earth to—'

'Keep calm and eat cake. Nobody ever died of embarrassment.'

Pretty sure she's wrong on that one. Somebody must have, somewhere in the world, what with all the younger bruvs around. Though I do take up her offer of cake. Then realize it's beetroot and chuck it in the bin.

I push open the door to our bedroom, which is met with some resistance due to Fred's pile of dinosaurs.

The sun takes up 99.8% of all the mass in our solar system, just .2% is planets and everything else. That ratio is a pretty accurate representation of our bedroom. Nowhere are the differences between me and my brother more noticeable than in the room we have to share. The room that's mainly dinosaurs and pants, held together by bogies.

Dad always says: '*IT'S FINE TO BE DIFFERENT. BROTHERS ARE MUCH LIKE CHEESE. THEY COME IN ALL SHAPES AND SIZES, OFTEN A BIT STINKY, AND SOME MORE MATURE THAN OTHERS, BUT TOGETHER THEY COMPLEMENT EACH OTHER TO MAKE UP A VARIED CHEESE BOARD. YOUR UNCLE RAY IS AN ACQUIRED TASTE, A GOATS' CHEESE, WHEREAS I'M MORE OF A—*'

'CHEESE STRING,' Mum always decides.

Fred is a smelly blue cheese that leaves a waft wherever he's been.

'Woah! What are you doing, Fred?' He's tipped out all the drawers under my desk.

'I need my crafty stuff!' He stamps his foot.

Fred hoards all the recycling so he can build rubbish dinosaurs. Literally. I pull out a box from the wardrobe full of paper and loo rolls and sit down beside him.

'Cuddle!' he yells, falling on top of me.

'Steady Freddie! What you up to anyway?'

'I'm making a poster for the moo-seum. Can you write on it *SAVE THE RORY?*'

'I think you owe me an apology first—the girlfriend thing this afternoon?'

'Flossie Mageggor made me say it.'

'Did she now . . .' I'm starting to wonder what she's got against me. Did I accidentally loot her treasure? 'Give it here then.'

'You're my favourite bruv.' He kisses my eye.

'I'm your only bruv, Fred, let's be honest.'

STANLEY'S UNIVERSAL TIPS

HOW TO STOP THE SPREAD OF 'BROTHER', IF YOU SHARE A ROOM

Make a line down the middle of EVERYTHING with masking-tape—walls, floors, windows, and, yes, the ceiling. If anything encroaches on your side, put it in a bin liner and request it

MY GENERAL STATE OF MIND

OVER THE MOON

SUNNY

CALM

OK

PHEW

NOT OK

ALARMED

NEED CAKE

STORMY

BLACK HOLE OF DOOM

gets shoved in the loft, quoting the Human Rights Act 1998, stating your parents have to comply with the Convention, and your right to peacefully enjoy your own property. (Mum: 'PRETTY SURE FRED CAN COME RIGHT BACKATCHA WITH THE HUMAN RIGHTS ACT 1998, AND THE RIGHT TO HAVE FREEDOM OF EXPRESSION, PICKLE-POPS.')

And while we're at it, I feel we need to tackle the bogey issue right here, right now.

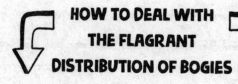

HOW TO DEAL WITH THE FLAGRANT DISTRIBUTION OF BOGIES

'PICKING THE NOSE IS MUCH LIKE CLEARING THE LOFT. IT SHOULD BE DONE WHEN NO ONE'S AROUND SO YOU CAN GET RIGHT INTO THE CORNERS AND GET SHOT OF ALL THE RUBBISH.'

Unfortunately, Fred never takes Dad's advice. So in the very likely event your younger brother comes into contact with your possessions, specify that he wears thick padded ski gloves. This will prevent him from picking his nose and:

EATING it.

WIPING it under your pillow.

WIPING it on your Death Star.

WIPING it all over your school project on trees (Mum: 'AT LEAST IT LOOKS LIKE A LEAF').

STICKING it back up his nose—it never fits, and will invariably fall out in your drink at teatime when he's leaning over to show you all the food inside his mouth.

None of this should have to be witnessed by anyone in the history of humankind <u>EVER</u>.

⤷ PARTY PLANNER

'Do I REALLY have to stay?'

'Fred's been shampooing his toys and blocked the plughole with dinosaur fluff,' sighs Mum, holding a plunger over her shoulder. 'It's an indoor ocean just waiting to happen.'

I'd sooner deal with that than Flossie's fifth birthday party. I can't believe Mum's making me take Fred AND stay. I'll definitely be needing my noise-cancelling headphones. And a GIANT lie-down when I get home. In this situation, you need something more substantial than just your **DAY-OUT-WITH-A-BRUV SURVIVAL KIT.**

MY GENERAL STATE OF MIND

OVER THE MOON

SUNNY

CALM

OK

PHEW

NOT OK

ALARMED

NEED CAKE

STORMY

BLACK HOLE OF DOOM

SMALL-YEAR-OLD PARTY PLANNER DOS AND DON'TS

DO

☆ find a wormhole so you can travel forward in time and miss the whole thing.

DON'T

☆ **JOIN IN ANY PARTY GAMES**—you'll easily win and have fifteen small-year-olds following you around until you share your prize with them. Which is a fun-size Milky Way.

☆ **HIDE UNDER THE TABLE**—where all the sulkers end up who get kicked out of pass-the-parcel early on, we're talking Snot, Tears, Tantrums— the Triangle of Ew.

☆ **ARRIVE EARLY**—you'll be 'volunteered' to mind the Bobbing for a Quality Street Paddling Pool, with just a pair of wet jeans and a soggy strawberry cream to show for it.

☆ **LEAVE LATE**—you'll be sucked into the 'tidy-up' vortex, which is basically scraping the buffet off the carpet and the cat.

☆ **TOUCH THE BUFFET**—*EVERYTHING* will have

already been touched, licked, chewed, sucked, and put back by the bogey-infested hands of fifteen small-year-olds.

We arrive fashionably five minutes late. Surprise, surprise, it's pirate-themed. Flossie's parents have stuck cardboard to a skip in the front garden and decorated it like a galleon that quite frankly looks like it sank 200 years ago. Eyepatched Flossie is stood inside it, shouting: 'Ahoy landlubbers!'

'So you're definitely five today?' I say, thinking if she lived on **PLUTO** she'd have to survive 1,240 years to reach her fifth birthday.

'That it be, yer lily-livered heave-ho.'

She does the eye-watching thing again which unnerves me to my core. I quickly walk inside and put on my headphones. There are plenty of lost adults wandering about, all staring enviously at my ear-gear. I spot a swing chair in the garden, currently occupied

OVER THE MOON

SUNNY

CALM

OK

PHEW

NOT OK

ALARMED

NEED CAKE

STORMY

BLACK HOLE OF DOOM

MY GENERAL STATE OF MIND

by nine kids. Flossie's teenage brother is on the barbecue. Not literally on it, that would be cannibalism.

Fred starts licking the crisps on the buffet so I quickly lower my headphones.

'Oh no, you're not doing that again.'

My phrase is echoed by someone stood next to me who's pulling away the arm of a little girl licking chocolate off the biscuits.

It's Jess. We roll eyes at each other, but she's soon distracted by three other small-year-olds picking things off the chocolate pirate ship.

'Quick everyone! Into the garden immediately.' Jess herds them away from the buffet. 'There's a piñata! Bashing and sweets!'

'Well played,' I nod.

'You gotta get them outside A-SAP, right?' she grabs a couple of cokes and a tube of Pringles. 'Come on, swing chair's free now.'

We watch them trying to hit a pirate ship piñata, blindfolded, with a big pointy stick. That recipe for disaster speaks for itself.

'So . . . you still looking for SWAT Team

members?' She offers me a crisp.

'I am as it happens.'

'I'll do it.'

'Really?' I say, spiffing out crisps, one of which lands on her jumper, and I immediately feel the effects of a Level Two humiliation.

'Well there's a telescope up for grabs isn't there?' She blows the crisp crumb away, obviously a pro in the getting spiffed with crisps business.

'I didn't realize you were into space.' And then I remember her reading the constellations book the other day—she should have been top of my list.

'If it's in a book I know about it. And I don't mind you didn't ask me,' she shrugs. 'Used to being overlooked. Call it middle sibling syndrome.'

'Oh. Sorry.'

''S'OK. What you thinking? Moon and tides? Solar eclipse?'

'I'm thinking meteor craters.'

'Good call,' she nods, eating five Pringles at once.

MY GENERAL STATE OF MIND

OVER THE MOON
SUNNY
CALM
OK
PHEW
NOT OK
ALARMED
NEED CAKE
STORMY
BLACK HOLE OF DOOM

'Although we can't enter unless there's four of us.' I try to do the same but end up with most of them on my lap.

'I can bring in Gemma. She doesn't know much about space, but is big on enthusiasm.'

'First SWAT Team get-together Monday?' I suggest. 'I'll drag Liam along, he owes me.'

He doesn't owe me, but it sort of sounds cool. What isn't cool is sneezing six times when Jess's cat jumps on my lap resulting in me throwing coke all over my jeans, and flinging the tube of crisps a metre into the air so they all land in a flower bed. Luckily Flossie's screams take any attention away from me.

> GET OFF YER BILGE RATS!
> IT'S MY TURN!

She's skipped her place in the queue and is hitting everything but the piñata.

'Just need to sort this before it turns into Armageddon,' Jess says calmly, before jumping up, grabbing the stick and handing Flossie a sherbet dip, averting a tantrum and the loss of any dads.

As I walk indoors, I find Fred crying into his bowl of jelly.

'What's wrong bruv?' I grab some napkins to try and soak up the worst of it.

'I w-w-wanted a R-R-R-Rory party,' he stutters, jelly falling out of his mouth. 'B-b-but he won't be alive none more!'

I'd forgotten he'd always wanted a dinosaur party at the museum. By the time his birthday comes around it'll be too late.

'Oh Fred, you still can.' There's nothing for it, it's time for the **SACRIFICE HUG**. And it's my favourite jumper. 'We'll do a Rory party at home. We can play pin the tail on the dinosaur, and Mum can make a, um, Gran can make a dinosaur cake. It'll be brilliant!'

I manage to calm him down—tricky when he's eaten his own weight in sugar. Which is why an hour later I'm stood in the hallway trying to drag Fred home. Even cake-on-a-stick won't

MY GENERAL STATE OF MIND

OVER THE MOON
SUNNY
CALM
OK
PHEW
NOT OK
ALARMED
NEED CAKE
STORMY
BLACK HOLE OF DOOM

work because he's overdosed on it.

'But my brother wants a party bag!' he keeps crying out to Flossie. 'He'll love it!'

'I'm not really into party bags . . .'

I blush, spotting Jess at the end of the hallway.

'I'm not into you!' Flossie declares stamping her foot. 'You don't deserve nuffink!'

And I can't say anything because her older brother is stood there with folded arms, his biceps bulging exactly as Liam described, looking me up and down as though I'M the baddie.

'Just banter!' I laugh nervously.

Flossie's mum comes running down the hall: 'It's OK! Maisy Watlington didn't show up, you can have hers. It's even got a yoyo in it! Would you like a balloon too, Stanley?'

'NO!' I shout a little too loudly, adding 'Thanks all the same . . .'

As we leave, Flossie does the eye-watching thing again.

'What IS it with her?' I mumble all the way home,

trying to hide the party bag I didn't want.

'She finks you're mean to me,' Fred mumbles through a mouthful of Smarties.

'I AM NOT!' I shout. 'I've just taken you to a party! I have to take you everywhere! And you constantly embarrass me and get me into trouble with your faffing about. Plus I have to share *EVERYTHING* with you, including your nose contents. It's not fair!'

Fred's bottom lip starts trembling and people are staring at us in the street.

'I told Flossie Mageggor you're not mean, even though sometimes you shout,' he sniffs. 'You're my ginormous bruvver.'

He always calls me that. Ironic seeing as I'm below average height.

'Don't worry, Stanley, I'll squeeze all the mad out of you,' he says, gripping me tightly.

'It's just . . . I really didn't want a party bag . . . that's all . . .'

Only I find out I really did. Inside there's a lenticular bookmark with JUPITER on it, which spins as you move it up and down.

OVER THE MOON

SUNNY

CALM

OK

PHEW

NOT OK

ALARMED

NEED CAKE

STORMY

BLACK HOLE OF DOOM

MY GENERAL STATE OF MIND

Fred was right. He knew I'd love it. Although the yoyo is absolute pants.

Eat humble pie. That's the only way to apologize in these circumstances. Told you I preferred cake to pie. But sometimes you gotta eat it up, even though it's hard to swallow. By the way, I don't mean eat an actual pie, I'm talking about apologizing.

'I was wrong, and you were right, and I'm really, really sorry Fred.'

'That's all right,' he smiles up at me, his teeth stained with Smarties. 'Now you can't be mad at me when you see your Death Star.'

I get home to find he's taken most of it apart in an attempt to build a **STEGGYSAURUS**. He's lucky it's not a real-life Death Star or they'd have blown him up by now.

'Fred!' Mum calls from the bathroom. 'Come and brush your teeth!'

'Freddie Fox is not here,' he yells back. 'Please leave a message after the beep . . . BEEEEEEEP!'

'Hi Frederick, this is Mum.' She's now stood in the doorway. 'If you get this message can you please come to the bathroom or I'm going to take your dinosaurs and very *slowly* chop their heads off.'

I've never seen him move so fast.

'Fred!' I yell with despair. 'That's MY toothbrush!'

'It's good to share,' he smiles through a mouthful of froth, chewing my toothbrush till it resembles roadkill hedgehog.

'No it isn't. That's just a myth sold to you by parents.'

OVER THE MOON

SUNNY

CALM

OK

PHEW

NOT OK

ALARMED

NEED CAKE

STORMY

BLACK HOLE OF DOOM

MY GENERAL STATE OF MIND

STANLEY'S UNIVERSAL TIPS

SHARING AND OTHER MYTHS

'When there's only one chocolate left, Mum's going to make it fair by eating it herself.'

Who said sharing was a good idea? Parents who never share anything at all, that's who. Sharing is overrated along with patience and cabbage. From a health and safety point of view, the following items should be a no-share area:

o **DREAMS**—the dinosaur dream explanation goes on for six days and you'll mummify from the boredom.

o **PILLOWS**—a new branch of biology could stem from the microorganisms found on the surface.

o **HARMONICAS**—let's be honest, it's more dribble than harmonica.

o **ROLL-ON DEODORANT**—because as Fred's discovered, it's a great way to pick up bed crumbs.

o **A MILKSHAKE WITH TWO STRAWS**—I've got one word for you: backwash.

⤷ PROMISES

'Good job I've just made two dozen cupcakes!'

Gran has agreed to take us to the museum so Fred can drop off his poster and I can do some research for Operation SWAT.

'What say we get rid of this and you trot along like a grandson should?' Gran unties the scarf from Fred's arm once we're out of Mum's view.

'I don't think that's a good idea,' I frown.

Whenever we go anywhere Mum straps Fred to her arm with a scarf, because he legs it if given half the chance. And Mum can't catch him up unless she abandons her flip-flops.

'Listen, I was one of eight—we skipped five miles to school and back without the need of scarves,' Gran winks.

'Can I run all the way to the moo-seum?'

MY GENERAL STATE OF MIND

OVER THE MOON
SUNNY
CALM
OK
PHEW
NOT OK
ALARMED
NEED CAKE
STORMY
BLACK HOLE OF DOOM

Freddie's eyes have lit up at the prospect of freedom.

'You don't even know the way, Fred,' I tut.

'What you *CAN* do, Freddie Fox, is run all the way to that postbox and count how many hands high it is.' Gran points.

He's so excited he can't get off the spot for a few seconds like Scooby-Doo.

'You do know he grabs the footstool in the living room,' I say as we watch him race into the distance, 'which he balances on top of the table so he can reach the biscuits off the shelf?'

'You can't knock all the craftiness out of him. He's a Fox after all.'

'It's more hands than I've got, Gran!' he laughs as we arrive at the postbox.

'Right answer!' she says, rewarding him with a cupcake. 'Now see that bench up ahead? Go and count how many bums wide it is.'

He can't wait to find out, and by the time we catch him up he proudly announces: 'It's six of my bums with room for your big one, Gran!'

Gran is some kind of magician. I make mental

notes to use this technique instead of the scarf—I'm fed up with being taken for a walk.

'Onwards Fred! To the bus stop! Count how much chewing gum is stuck under the seats, bonus points for pink.'

Genius, if a little bit gross.

His little legs are running out of puff now, and he's still counting by the time we reach him.

'Ten . . . eleventeen . . . tooty-three . . . there's four!'

'Magnificent! Now, see the church? There'll be loads of confetti on the pathway—'

'Oh but I'm missing you, Gran,' he sighs, taking hold of her ring-bedecked hand. 'Can I stay with you and sing my song about Rory?'

'Course you can.' She mops his brow and pulls out a juice carton.

If I hadn't just witnessed it, I'd have never believed it. Fred has never asked to hold anyone's hand. All she needs now is a tactic to stop him singing 'The Rory Song'—all twenty verses with harmonica interlude.

OVER THE MOON

SUNNY

CALM

OK

PHEW

NOT OK

ALARMED

NEED CAKE

STORMY

BLACK HOLE OF DOOM

MY GENERAL STATE OF MIND

Time for noise-cancelling headphones as we pass the church and turn right into Parks Road. We reach the museum, and Fred jumps across the giant dinosaur footprints that are stretched across the front lawn like stepping stones.

RECIPE FOR DISASTER

1 Harmonica
1 Bruv who can't actually play the harmonica

Take my advice and don't mix

I notice a large banner above the oak doors:

Leave the Right Kind of Footprint Behind—New Exhibition Opening Soon!

Stood beneath it is the protestor bloke off the telly, with a small group of people holding 'Save Rory' signs. I lower my headphones as he approaches Gran.

'The name's Noke, Jim Noke.' He holds out a pen. 'Would you like to sign our petition to save Rory?'

'I will, Noke Jim Noke!'

SAVE RORY

Freddie shouts.

'Oh, I'm sorry young man, you're far too young.'

'Mr Smelly Pants Rhinoceros!' Fred sticks out his tongue.

'Fred! Say sorry!' I shake my head in shame.

'I've had worse.'

'Well you may not be a smelly pants rhinoceros,' Gran says, 'but it seems daft kids can't sign it. I'll sign on your behalf, Fred.'

'We were hoping for a bit more support after our stint on the news.' He straightens his tie. 'Of course in our day there wasn't all this newfangled climate change nonsense.'

'It's not nonsense,' I mumble, hoping all the recycling I've had to take out over the years is not a complete waste of my time.

We pass through the doors, up the stone steps and into reception. It's overrun with small-year-olds, and their parents muttering, 'MIGHT BE THE LAST

OVER THE MOON

SUNNY

CALM

OK

PHEW

NOT OK

ALARMED

NEED CAKE

STORMY

BLACK HOLE OF DOOM

MY GENERAL STATE OF MIND

CHANCE YOU GET TO SEE HIM', '*BUT YOU'VE JUST BEEN TO THE TOILET*', and '*WILL YOU PLEASE STOP LICKING THE CABINET?*'

'Morning, boys! I've got a brand new quiz today!' Mary waves enthusiastically at us.

'Oh, we won't be needing that,' I say with a bit too much relief in my voice, as Freddie stands on his tiptoes to hand in his picture.

'*SAVE THE RORY?*' Mary reads aloud. 'I'm afraid we won't be able to put this up. Museum policy.'

'That's a point of view, and everyone's allowed one of them,' Gran frowns.

'Of course, madam,' Mary laughs nervously. 'But if you just cut the slogan off the top—'

'I'm not chopping up my grandson's picture! It's a masterpiece!' Gran takes it back. 'I want to speak to the manager.'

Fred's bottom lip starts to wobble as Mary pulls out a radio, fumbling with the buttons: 'Mayday, mayday, come in Rex Watch, we have a Code Silver, with blue highlights, complaining at reception, please report right now. Thanks, um, over.'

'*COPY THAT, EAGLE EYES, I'M ON MY WAY*

OVER, OVER.'

Within a minute Mr Hadfield appears, clipping his radio back on to his belt.

'It's another pro-dinosaur poster.' Mary gestures to the picture, then fans her face with her quiz sheets. 'Sorry, Mr Hadfield, but I'm not cut out for confrontation.'

'I'm afraid Mr Banner won't let us put them up.' Mr Hadfield turns to Gran. 'Apologies, to you and your delightful children.'

'Oh behave yourself! They're my grandkids!' Gran chuckles.

'Anyway, I'm sorry to say Rory's on his way out. And I've got fifty-five new facts to learn or I'm on my way out too.'

'And me.' Mary is now furiously sharpening pencils. 'I mean, is the future about upcycling or recycling, I can never remember.'

'Can't WE have Rory, Mister Bushy Eyebrows?' Fred pipes up. 'Put him in our living room?'

'Not unless your household contents insurance covers a sixty-five-million-year-old

MY GENERAL STATE OF MIND

OVER THE MOON
SUNNY
CALM
OK
PHEW
NOT OK
ALARMED
NEED CAKE
STORMY
BLACK HOLE OF DOOM

T-rex,' Mr Hadfield comments. 'And you haven't got a ceiling in your living room.'

Freddie looks up at Gran for an answer.

'Well it had one last time I looked, love.'

'Can I interest you in our amazing scale model?' interrupts a short man with a very neat beard. 'John Banner. You probably saw me on the news. Walk this way and I'll be able to point out all the exciting wonders of our future exhibition.'

He leads a group of us over to a miniature white sculpture where a reporter is taking pictures and scribbling down notes. It's dotted with labels saying stuff like SUPER INTERACTIVE TABLETS, FUN EXPERIMENTS, and MORE FUN EXPERIMENTS, and in the middle, a white ball dominates the whole thing.

'What's that?' Fred points, lightly touching it until I quickly pull his hand away.

'Why that, young sir, is Earth.'

'But Earth's got blue bits.'

'Of course! This is just a model. The globe will be the centre of our exhibition, on which we will project melting ice caps, disappearing coastlines, endangered animals. And it's all about footprints! We hope to inspire people to reduce their carbon footprint. After all, the only prints we should leave behind are ones in the sand . . .' He winks at the reporter.

'Stinky footprints.' Fred folds his arms.

'Hands up who wants to make a rain gauge?' Mr Banner laughs nervously.

'A wot, mister?' asks a boy with one eye on the stuffed badger (and who can blame him).

'Or a bag out of a T-shirt? Because they're just SOME of the exciting activities we'll be offering when we reopen!' he tries to say over Fred's raspberries that he's now blowing.

'That's not exciting,' Fred stamps his foot. 'Rory's exciting. He's a dinosaur that lived gajillions of years ago with teeth the size of narnas and I wish he'd eat you up!'

Narna teeth

OVER THE MOON

SUNNY

CALM

OK

PHEW

NOT OK

ALARMED

NEED CAKE

STORMY

BLACK HOLE OF DOOM

MY GENERAL STATE OF MIND

'These super interactive tablets?' I ask, taking out a lollipop and shoving it in Fred's gob. 'Are they for everyone to use?'

'Yes! It's all state-of-the-art technology.'

'Well that's fine and dandy,' Gran snorts. 'But why get rid of the dinosaur? Because he's old and past it? Over the hill? Are you ageist, young man?'

'Don't be absurd, madam!' He slicks his hair back. 'Mr Hadfield! Tell them some of your new facts.'

'Righto . . . um . . . I . . . haven't quite learnt them all yet,' he says, fumbling with his notes.

'Can we have a photograph by the stuffed badger?' asks the reporter. 'Favourite of mine.'

'Of course,' and he glares back at Fred. 'Absolutely *NO* touching!'

'I wanna see Rory,' Fred pleads.

'Go on then,' I say, which is my cue to find facts for Operation SWAT. 'Gran, did you know that the Arizona crater is nearly one mile wide, created by a giant meteor which exploded on impact?'

But before she can be amazed, we both jump at a sudden anguished yell.

'WHERE HAS EARTH GONE?'

I spin round and Mr Banner is flapping about the cabinets.

'Mr Hadfield! Have you seen Earth?' he gasps.

'Aren't we on it, spinning around the sun at thirty kilometres a second?' Mr Hadfield says, remembering one of his new facts.

'Not ACTUAL Earth! MODEL Earth!' Mr Banner cries, pointing to the exhibition plans.

Mr Hadfield pulls out his radio: 'We have a Code, um, Model Earth Disaster. Block all exits, over.'

'Oh! What should I do?' Mary jumps up and grabs the tub of pencils. 'I'm totally untrained for this, Mr Hadfield!'

I peek my head around the column, and sure enough the white ball has gone. My instinct is to quickly check for Fred. He's not by Rory. My heart does a flutter. The sort of flutter that tells you your little brother is involved in all this and if you don't sort it out guess who's going to get told off.

'Gran! Fred's gone AWOL! Protect the exit, I'll check the rest of the museum.'

'Say no more,' she pulls a cupcake out of her bag. 'Hopefully the smell will entice him out.'

There's no sign of him anywhere. Not by the stuffed badger. And thankfully not by the fragile wasps' nest.

'Toilets!' I say under my breath. Perhaps he needed a wee, and is innocent in all this. Yeah right. He never goes on his own due to the lav-lav snakes. I rush into the men's, and spot him in a cubicle frantically flushing.

'Everything all right?' I approach hesitantly, hoping I'm not about to see what I'm about to see.

'It won't go,' he says grumpily. 'I tried eleventeen times, but it's too hunourmous.'

He's trying to flush Earth down the toilet.

'Well no wonder our planet's going down the pan, the way you treat it! That's where we're going to end up if we don't all start recycling RIGHT

AWAY!' I whisper-shout. 'Mr Banner's going nuts in there! We've got to put this back or I'm in BIG trouble, and you will be too.'

'But if we flush it away, they can't get rid of Rory.'

'It doesn't work like that, Fred.'

I grab some paper towels and ickily pick the floating ball out of a thankfully clean toilet pan. Of course in reality only **SATURN** would float as it's the least dense. If you could find a toilet pan big enough. I dry it up as best I can, and wash my hands three times.

'You need to cause a distraction so I can replace **EARTH**.'

'Shall I be Wee Willie Winkie?'

'Um, best not . . .'

It's hard to prepare for these kind of moments, you just have to improvise, but remember, Wee Willie Winkie is NEVER an option. I whisper the plan as we head back into the hall. I can still hear yelling, with Mr Hadfield using his torch in broad daylight.

'Remember?' I say to Fred. 'On three . . .'

OVER THE MOON

SUNNY

CALM

OK

PHEW

NOT OK

ALARMED

NEED CAKE

STORMY

BLACK HOLE OF DOOM

MY GENERAL STATE OF MIND

He nods.

'Three!'

I'M A BOUNDY GAZELLE!

he shouts, jumping all around the fragile wasps' nest.

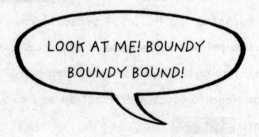

LOOK AT ME! BOUNDY BOUNDY BOUND!

'Absolutely no bounding allowed around the fragile wasps' nest!' Mr Hadfield orders.

The distraction is enough for me to quickly put Earth back on its spot, albeit slightly mucky with a dent in the top. At least it's now a more accurate representation.

I grab Fred's hand.

'We're leaving. Sorry Mr Hadfield, he had three bowls of Chocco Pops this morning.'

We charge out of the oak doors with Gran, just as Mr Banner exclaims: 'It's back! Ew! What on *EARTH* has happened to Earth?'

When we're out of earshot I take out the wet wipes and clean Fred up.

'Don't ever try to flush Earth down the toilet again, you hear me?'

'Why not?' he pouts.

'Because I said so!' I stand wagging my finger at him.

I've actually turned into Dad at the age of eleven. His bottom lip trembles, so I whip out the tea towel and bring him in for a hug.

'I know you want to save Rory, but I reckon you've got to learn to embrace change. You know, like it says on Mum's fridge magnets—'

SAVE THE RORY! SAVE THE RORY!

I'm interrupted by chanting. It's Gran, having accosted Mr Noke's megaphone in

MY GENERAL STATE OF MIND

OVER THE MOON

SUNNY

CALM

OK

PHEW

NOT OK

ALARMED

NEED CAKE

STORMY

BLACK HOLE OF DOOM

exchange for cupcakes.

'Rory's not over the hill yet!' she yells, jumping along the dinosaur footprints waving Fred's poster.

I'm keen to scarper in case Mr Banner's worked out what's happened to Earth. But Fred joins in as the reporter takes pictures of the protest.

'Do you like the new exhibition plans?' she asks him, scribbling away on her pad.

'No. I tried to flush it down the—'

'SAVE THE RORY!' I yell to drown out his revelation, and unwittingly have my picture taken too.

Cut to next day's local newspaper:

'I love dinosaurs!' grins nine-year-old Stanley Box, as he stands in protest with his brother Freddie over the removal of Rory the T-rex. Their campaign 'Save the Rory' drew a small crowd at the weekend, and as Freddie, age five, revealed: 'My brother's going to help me save him, cos he promised.'

For the record, I did not say I loved dinosaurs. And I'm actually eleven. And they got my name wrong. And, hang on a minute, I never promised anything of the sort.

OVER THE MOON

SUNNY

CALM

OK

PHEW

NOT OK

ALARMED

NEED CAKE

STORMY

BLACK HOLE OF DOOM

MY GENERAL STATE OF MIND

⤷ YOU SHOULD KNOW BETTER

About one hundred tonnes of space dust falls to Earth every day. I wish some of it would land on Liam's head right now.

'That's stupiculous!' Liam has brought the newspaper cutting to school and pinned it up on the noticeboard. 'Fancy getting papped like that. Tragic.'

'All right, leave it out. It's bad enough Fred thinks I'm going to save Rory.'

'I don't have a younger sibling, as you know,' Liam says. 'But even one of your Stan-tastic diagrams isn't gonna help you with that.'

'Why are you saving a dinosaur anyway? I mean, he's like, well old,' Idris points out the completely obvious.

'Didn't you used to have a dinosaur duvet Liam?' I try to deflect the banter away from me.

'No way!' he protests. 'I only have, like, cool things.'

'Yeah, you did!' Idris remembers. 'It had a diplosaurus on!'

'It was a diplodocus you numpty!' His face flushes when he realizes he's owned up to it. 'It wasn't mine! Shut up!'

'The diplodocus info goes no further if you help me with the science fair,' I whisper.

'That is bribe-mail, bro, total mate treason.'

'So, when pressure builds in the magma chamber, we have what is known as a volcanic eruption,' explains Mr Fisher pointing at the whiteboard.

JUPITER'S moon, Io, erupts lava fountains up to 400 kilometres high. I can't help noticing how similar a volcanic eruption is to my brother's toxic guffs, and sort of go a bit off-topic:

OVER THE MOON

SUNNY

CALM

OK

PHEW

NOT OK

ALARMED

NEED CAKE

STORMY

BLACK HOLE OF DOOM

MY GENERAL STATE OF MIND

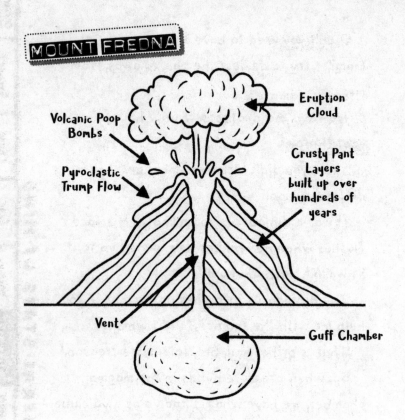

MOUNT FREDNA

Eruption Cloud

Volcanic Poop Bombs

Pyroclastic Trump Flow

Crusty Pant Layers built up over hundreds of years

Vent

Guff Chamber

'Mount Fredna's unlikely to be dormant any time soon,' I whisper to Liam who's trying to alert me to the teacher behind my chair.

'Guff chamber?' Mr Fisher roars, jabbing his finger on my diagram. 'Tell me, Mr Fox, what has THAT got to do with Mount Etna?'

'Um, nothing Mr Fisher,' I gulp. 'But did you know that the largest volcano in our solar system is on MARS?'

Liam holds his head in his hands at my attempt to impress our weary teacher.

'If you kept yourself firmly rooted to EARTH, Mr Fox, you might actually finish one of my lessons. Reflection sheet at morning break,' he says with gritted teeth.

'Oh, but I've got a top secret strategy session with Operation SWAT, sir.'

I immediately realize I've said those words out loud as I hear the rest of the class sniggering.

'Well now you've got a session with Operation Reflection Sheet.'

It means my fellow teammates have to skip lunch break, which is not great for group morale.

'I hope you at least managed to bring Liam on board seeing as I'm missing out on book club,' Jess grumbles as she clears the whiteboard for me. 'If I don't get my five chapters a day I feel seriously malnourished.'

Liam's timing could not have been worse. We look out the window to see him squashing his nose against the glass like a demented pig-boy.

MY GENERAL STATE OF MIND

OVER THE MOON

SUNNY

CALM

OK

PHEW

NOT OK

ALARMED

NEED CAKE

STORMY

BLACK HOLE OF DOOM

I roll my eyes and open the window: 'Hey, remember that duvet you once had, Liam?'

'Hey, remember that time you got stuck in the lame baby swings? There's no way I'm doing science at lunchtime, so don't go all "Operation Navy Seals" on me,' he quotes with his fingers.

'Just stop right there!' says a voice belonging to Gemma as she flounces into the classroom and whomps her rucksack on the desk. 'I'd rather be out in the sunshine too, but I know this team won't win without me. Only I can bring the ideas, the talent, and, let's face it, modern street dance to this outfit. So I suggest we audition Liam right now because I can't teach slackers.'

'Gemma,' Jess interrupts. 'It's a science fair, not an X FACTOR performance.'

'LIFE is a performance, Jess. We all play roles, and mine is to ensure we drag science fairs into the twenty-first century. I've already choreo-graphed the Comet Swagger Rap.'

I put my hand up. 'Um, we're doing meteorites, not comets.'

'I'm not doing nothing.' Liam goes to close the

window.

'Look,' Jess walks over, holding up a Victoria sandwich. 'I've brought cake.'

'Woah . . .' he climbs into the classroom.

Of course. The power of cake. Now everyone's listening, I pick up a whiteboard marker.

'Tonnes of meteors fall to Earth every day.' I draw a big circle and bombard it with pen strokes. 'Most are dust from comet tails and asteroids, and nearly all of them burn up in our atmosphere creating fiery trails, or shooting stars. But we're interested in the ones that fall to Earth.'

'Oh look, it's Professor Brian Cox.' Liam rolls his eyes while gobbling cake.

'Ssshhhh!' Jess waves him out of the way.

OVER THE MOON
SUNNY
CALM
OK
PHEW
NOT OK
ALARMED
NEED CAKE
STORMY
BLACK HOLE OF DOOM

MY GENERAL STATE OF MIND

'Stan's just getting to the good bit.'

'He is?' Liam curls his lip.

'Yes I am actually.' I get my crater factsheet out and clear my throat. 'The meteor that made Popigai Crater in Siberia created diamonds on impact; the Spider Crater in Australia does actually look like a spider; and get this—the impact crater under the sea off the coast of Mexico is about sixty-five million years old. And what happened *SIXTY-FIVE MILLION YEARS AGO*?'

'You started this conversation?' Liam rolls his eyes.

'Actually, an asteroid the size of a small city hit Earth and wiped out the dinosaurs. Impact craters tell us all this because they're amazing, and guess what? We're going to make them!'

Jess claps enthusiastically as Liam groans.

'OMG!' Gemma jumps up. 'Maybe we could have a dance battle between the dinos and the comets— prehistoric urban freestyling!'

'METEORITES!' I shout. 'And we don't need urban freestyling when we've got this.'

I take out a perspex box containing my birthday

present from Gran last year.

'Is that a REAL meteorite?' Jess gasps.

'Yep. And hopefully it's going to impress the judges too. Because I've drawn up a diagram.'

'I'd have been disappointed if you hadn't.' Liam helps himself to more cake as I unfold my grand plan:

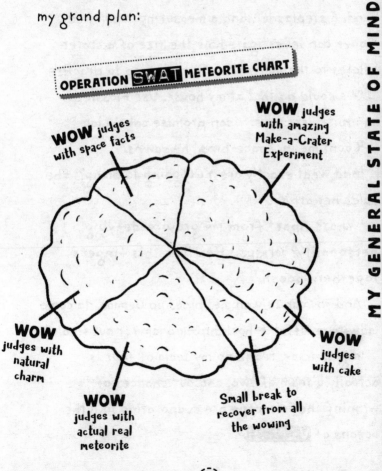

OPERATION SWAT METEORITE CHART

WOW judges with space facts

WOW judges with amazing Make-a-Crater Experiment

WOW judges with natural charm

WOW judges with cake

WOW judges with actual real meteorite

Small break to recover from all the wowing

'That is *WAY* too much wowing,' Liam immediately points out.

'We're going to need *LOADS* of accessories.' Gemma starts making a list. 'Bandanas, glitter, comet tails . . .'

'Um, no, just pretend meteorites, buckets of sand, a stepladder, and a measuring tape,' I say. 'So we can investigate how the size of a crater relates to the meteorite. And we need to practise.'

'We could do that at my house. Use Flossie's sandpit,' Jess says. 'I can promise cake, Liam.'

'Count me in, space-bros,' he yawns.

'And what exactly are *YOU* going to bring?' She folds her arms.

'What? Apart from my gravity-defying personality? Crisps.' He flicks his fingers together. 'Boosh.'

'And you can rely on me,' pipes up Gemma, 'to come up with an off-the-hook hip-hop jam for our finale.'

'Right,' I say, realizing my team of four is actually a team of two, and our chances of winning the telescope are evaporating like the oceans of VENUS.

I cycle home with Liam to find a police car pulled up outside our home.

'What's Fred done now?' Liam tuts.

'Dunno . . .' I frown, wondering if he's been borrowing packets of biscuits from the corner shop again.

I rush in to find two police officers stood in the lounge, Mum looking furious with her hands on her hips, and Fred looking sheepish, curled up on the sofa sucking his thumb.

'Everything all right?' I gulp.

'No. Everything's very much *NOT* all right,' Mum frowns. 'Believe me, Mum is trying to remain calm, but Mum o'clock can't come quick enough. Can you explain to my son what this is all about, officers?'

'Certainly ma'am,' one of the police officers says, opening up his notepad. 'We attended Camford Museum this morning, whereupon we met with Mr John Banner, to examine CCTV

MY GENERAL STATE OF MIND

OVER THE MOON | SUNNY | CALM | OK | PHEW | NOT OK | ALARMED | NEED CAKE | STORMY | BLACK HOLE OF DOOM footage from Sunday just gone. It appears that Frederick Fox removed Earth and attempted to flush it down the toilet. He also disturbed the museum's prized fragile wasps' nest which now needs conservation work.'

'Can I just confirm,' Mum says calmly, 'that Earth is a *PAPER BALL*?'

'A styrofoam ball, ma'am, which was atop a mini architectural sculpture costing approximately,' he reads from his notebook, 'five hundred pounds.'

Blimey. I could have made it with the contents of Fred's crafty-stuff box.

'So when exactly did this happen, Stanley?' Mum taps her foot and purses her lips. 'Because in all honesty, you really are old enough to know better than to take Fred anywhere near a mini architectural sculpture worth five hundred pounds.'

'When we went with Gran,' I squeak, pulling at a thread on the sofa.

'Ahhh!' Mum rolls her eyes. 'If Earth's going to be knocked off its axis by anyone, it'll be when Gran's about. I can only apologize, officers. Can we pay it back in instalments?'

'I'm afraid that isn't all, ma'am,' says the other police officer opening up her notepad.

'Oh good gracious, what now?'

'After viewing further CCTV footage it seems a T-rex was, ahem, coloured in. With crayons.'

'Crayons? I thought we'd banished those evil things?' Mum's voice is now wavering between tears and mad laughter.

'Rory's old and needs my help!' Fred stands up on the sofa to plead his case. 'I was just trying to make him feel better! He's all grey and alone. And now he's gonna die all over again!'

'Can I just confirm—Rory IS the T-rex?' The police officer is poised with her notepad and pen.

'Yes,' Mum sighs. 'So how much do we owe, officers?'

'Mr Banner has decided to overlook these incidents if the Fox brothers agree to keep off the premises for the foreseeable.'

'Wos that mean?' Fred asks.

'It means we're banned. Banned from the

MY GENERAL STATE OF MIND

OVER THE MOON

SUNNY

CALM

OK

PHEW

NOT OK

ALARMED

NEED CAKE

STORMY

BLACK HOLE OF DOOM

museum,' I say, looking down at my feet.

'I can't ever see Rory for ever again?' Fred sniffs, his bottom lip poking out.

'Certainly looks that way,' Mum says. 'And to be honest I think it's for the best, Fred.'

'NO IT ISN'T!' he shouts, jumping up and down on the sofa and hurling sofa cushions. 'I WANNA SEE RORY!'

'Well you can't. We agree to Mr Banner's terms, officers. Is that all?'

As Mum shows them out, I try to hug Fred but he's curled up in a ball underneath the coffee table. I reach in and rub his teary cheek.

'I love him as much as b-b-biscuits. . .' he sobs.

'I know, bruv. I'm sorry.'

'What on earth will the neighbours think, having the police call on us?' Mum comes back in, picking up the cushions. 'I must say Mum is relieved at the museum's reaction, it could have cost us a fortune. However she's disappointed in you, Stanley. If you didn't go around with your head in the stars we might not get into situations like this. I expect it from Fred, but you're old enough to know better.'

SO UNFAIR, I say in my head. Even with my head in the stars I still managed to stop Earth from entering the sewer. And wiped off most of the crayon damage. Where was Mum? Oh yeah. Enjoying Mum o'clock.

And as for that worn-out saying. Hmmm . . .

Older siblings face that gem on an almost daily basis, and you know what? Here's the percentage breakdown regarding that statement:

ARE WE ACTUALLY OLD ENOUGH TO KNOW BETTER?

I don't actually know better

I have no influence over this situation at all even if I did or didn't know better

I do know better but I'm pretending I don't

I was in the toilet and honestly have no idea what just happened

OVER THE MOON

SUNNY

CALM

OK

PHEW

NOT OK

ALARMED

NEED CAKE

STORMY

BLACK HOLE OF DOOM

MY GENERAL STATE OF MIND

So, a more accurate statement would be: 'SOMETIMES YOU'RE OLD ENOUGH TO KNOW BETTER, BUT MORE OFTEN THAN NOT I REALIZE IT'S OUT OF YOUR CONTROL, AND TEN PER CENT OF THE TIME YOU'RE IN THE TOILET.'

⮡ BRUV TAG-ALONG

Every eleven years the sun flips upside down—its magnetic poles change places so that north becomes south, and south becomes north. Which is what must happen to Liam's navigation in a town he's lived in all his life.

'Sorry I'm late. Took a wrong turn,' he says scoffing Hula Hoops. 'Still, I brought crisps.'

'I've never been to Jess Mageggor's house before!' Fred says excitedly.

'Yes you have, it's Flossie's house. Look, there's the skip.'

'Well I definitely haven't!' Liam enthusiastically rings the doorbell.

I'm not sure what's worse, having to bring along my younger bruv or my mate who's just after more cake.

It's a well-known fact that if you're an older sibling, at some point your parents are going to ask you the following question: 'Oh, would you mind your brother tagging along? He won't be any trouble.' But trouble is exactly what he will be. They might as well be asking: 'You know that thing you've been looking forward to doing for ages? It's now going to be rubbish.'

IT'S BASICALLY THIS:

you are here

so is your
bruv

FUN

So if you're off to Jess McGregor's house for an Operation SWAT crater test with a bruv in tow, this is where you need the **DO-NOT-INTERRUPT KIT** which is basically a DVD and a bag of toffees— keeps brain and gob busy at the same time. Plus check his pockets to make sure he hasn't packed a harmonica, which I'm just hiding in my rucksack as Jess's older brother opens the door.

'Hi,' I say, sticking out my hand and hoping to make peace with his biceps. 'I don't think we've been formally introduced. Stan.'

He slips off his headphones and stares at my hand like it's made of jelly then looks back up at me.

'Is that a constellation of the **PLOUGH** on your—'

'Yes. Yes it is.' There's no way I'm arguing with him about constellations versus asterisms.

He shows us into the garden where Jess is raking Flossie's sandpit ready to make craters. Gemma's on the swing chair, surrounded by fabric.

MY GENERAL STATE OF MIND

OVER THE MOON · SUNNY · CALM · OK · PHEW · NOT OK · ALARMED · NEED CAKE · STORMY · BLACK HOLE OF DOOM

'Help yourself to snacks, and *PLAY NICELY*.'

'You're not Mum, Orson,' Jess frowns at him.

'I'm in charge today.' He points to his eyes and then at all of us. 'Don't make me send you to the naughty step.'

He heads back inside, jumping on the sofa to play his Xbox.

'He's *SO FABUCOOL*, isn't he?' Liam nudges me. 'Orson? I mean, that name is AMAZESOME. And did you see his trainers? Out of this world, man-bro. So where's the cake?'

'After the experiment. I've got to hold your attention somehow,' Jess says. 'Did you bring any pretend meteorites?'

'I brought crisps,' he shrugs.

'Don't worry, I've got loads,' I pour out a bag of apples, oranges, golf balls, and marbles on to the patio. 'And hope you don't mind, but I had to bring Fred too.'

'I'd be surprised if you didn't.' She hands him a paintbrush. 'Go and paint the fence, Fred.'

He doesn't need to be asked twice.

'Errr . . . paint?'

'It's just water,' Jess says. 'You have to be ten steps ahead. All they're about at that age is running around with no purpose.'

'Speaking of no purpose,' I whisper, 'what's Gemma doing exactly?'

'Making totally edgy comet tails.' She hands us each a belt draped with ribbons and tinsel. 'We're taking coolness to the max, people.'

'I'm not a comet,' I whisper, fastening my tail. 'I'm a meteorite.'

'Wos HE doing here?' Flossie appears with her arms folded and a pirate hat perched on her high hair.

'Flossie, shoo!' Jess waves her away.

'No.' She stamps her foot. 'Stanley made Fred get banned from the moo-seum. He can't see Rory for ever again.'

'Really?' Jess turns to look at me. 'Spill the beans, Stanley!'

'It's a long story.' I look down at my trainers. 'Beginning with Fred, and ending in him trying to flush a model Earth down the toilet. We're banned for ever.'

'You're an actual criminal?' Liam's mouth has dropped open.

'I'm not, he is!' I point to Fred.

'You have to make him *NOT* banned,' Flossie pouts. 'So he can see Rory before he dies.'

'He already *IS* dead. And I'm a little bit busy right now with Operation SWAT,' I say standing up to her. I won't be bullied by a five-year-old pirate. Except I've just made her really mad.

She runs towards me at full speed, arms spinning like windmills, bashing my legs.

'Floss! Get off!' Jess tries to drag her away. 'Orson! You need to sort her out!'

But he can't hear through his headphones.

'Oh those things are infuriating!' She stomps inside to the sofa and snaps them off his head.

'Woah! You nearly broke my babies!'

'Keep her under control! I watched her yesterday so you could do band practice.'

'He's in a band too?' Liam whispers, his eyes as wide as a full moon.

'Chillax, sis, I got this.' Orson beckons Flossie and Fred inside, handing them controllers. 'Come on, little dudes, let's race.'

Jess heads back into the garden to set up the stepladder.

'Sorry Stan.' She climbs the steps. 'She's been eating party leftovers.'

'Um, no worries,' I say, steadying the ladder. 'I THINK my legs are still working.'

'Can you believe I haven't read a book since yesterday?' she sighs. 'I try to do fun stuff with Flossie, but I don't want to stand in a skip all day calling the neighbours bilge rats.'

'It's like the Venn diagram we did at school.' I pass her a golf ball. 'Trying to find your common multiples.'

'If Orson was my brother, we'd have LOADS of common multiples,' Liam nods. 'The main one being, like, coolness. Chicka-wow!'

He fist bumps me and pulls away with a mimed exploding hand.

OVER THE MOON

SUNNY

CALM

OK

PHEW

NOT OK

ALARMED

NEED CAKE

STORMY

BLACK HOLE of DOOM

MY GENERAL STATE OF MIND

'Right Liam, I'm going to drop the golf ball into the sand,' Jess instructs. 'I want you to remove it carefully and measure the crater. Then Gemma, can you please write down the measurement?'

'I'm just bustin some moves, Jess.' She's freestyling round the garden with bits of tinsel in her hair. 'Crucial I express the elliptical orbit of the comet through krumping.'

'What's crucial is making sure we can interpret our experiment.' Jess is now dropping golf balls and oranges into the sand. 'Can you measure the craters, Liam?'

'I bet Orson's always sneaking out at night via a drainpipe,' he says dreamily.

'He doesn't live in a movie,' she tuts.

'If I had a bro, I would definitely choose Orson,' Liam whispers. 'He's, like, got the most brillendous hairstyle I've EVER seen.'

'Liam, can you just measure the—'

'And his T-shirts are unsurpassed on every level . . .'

'Yeah, but Liam, can you please—'

'And his man-jewellery!' he whistles. 'Can I

borrow your brother?'

'MEASURE THE CRATERS!' Jess yells and Liam jumps, snapping the tape measure shut on his thumb.

'Woah! Calm down! I nearly lost a hand there!'

And then I realize why he made the effort to turn up today. Not because of cake. Because of Orson. The chance to meet

THE BROTHER OF HIS DREAMS.

'This isn't going to work!' Jess cries, pulling off her comet tail. 'We were never going to get on! We're just not compatible! I quit!'

'Hey, what if Orson came on board? I bet WE'D be compatible.' Liam is oblivious to the frustration hovering above him on a stepladder.

'You know what, Liam?' Jess shouts down. 'The only thing you're compatible with is an amoeba!'

MY GENERAL STATE OF MIND

OVER THE MOON
SUNNY
CALM
OK
PHEW
NOT OK
ALARMED
NEED CAKE
STORMY
BLACK HOLE of DOOM

'That's a lot of angerment you got right there, Jess.' He shakes his head. 'Time for cake?'

Flossie and Fred have now rushed into the garden, taking advantage of the situation by chucking sand everywhere.

'Stop! You're ruining it!' Jess yells.

'Everything all right?' Even Orson has heard the outburst over his headphones. 'Am I gonna have to send someone to the naughty step?'

'I'll go.' Liam puts up his hand. 'If you want me to . . .?'

And then Flossie picks up a golf ball.

'No, Flossie!' shouts Jess.

Too late. She throws it right at me. I manage to swerve and watch it fly past an oblivious Liam, where it smashes straight through a window.

I left feeling lucky I only have ONE sibling. Poor Jess is in the middle of two, feeling invisible. What would it be like if I had a mainly horizontal teenager too? Trouble is, I keep dreaming about the perfect older brother. He'd not only be able to look after Fred every time Mum had to watch EastEnders, but obviously he'd be on the NASA Space Programme with room for me in his rocket.

And I'm pretty sure he'd be able to sort out the mess my SWAT Team are in, because my chances of winning a telescope have just exploded like **THE BIG BANG**.

OVER THE MOON

SUNNY

CALM

OK

PHEW

NOT OK

ALARMED

NEED CAKE

STORMY

BLACK HOLE OF DOOM

MY GENERAL STATE OF MIND

⤷ THE CONCEPT OF BORROWING

The pressure on JUPITER is so strong it squishes gas into liquid. It could crush a spaceship like a plastic cup. Which is what happens to my soul every time Fred asks to borrow something.

'Can I borrow your space book for Mrs Parker's sun lesson?' Fred is already holding it by the front door. 'I honestly won't lick it.'

Trouble is, when you look up the definition of borrow:

> **Borrow** To take something belonging to someone else with the intention of returning it

My brother's brilliant at the first part, not so much the second. So basically it's theft.

THINGS HE'S BORROWED BUT
NEVER RETURNED:

- **LEGO MOON BUGGY**—caught in a tree because he thought he could chuck it on the actual moon.
- **HELIUM BIRTHDAY BALLOON**—'oops, it haxidentally let go of my finger'.
- **MY DIGNITY**—let's not forget the picnic at the park incident.

THINGS HE'S BORROWED AND
RETURNED THAT I WISH HE HADN'T:

- **SPACE PEN**—chewed and shoved up his nose.
- **MY HAIRBRUSH**—sprinkled with nits.
- **LIQUORICE ALLSORTS**—technically you can't really borrow sweets, but that didn't stop him spitting them out and handing them back.

'I need it today, Fred, sorry. Take an orange instead. I promise it'll come in handy for the solar eclipse.'

MY GENERAL STATE OF MIND

OVER THE MOON
SUNNY
CALM
OK
PHEW
NOT OK
ALARMED
NEED CAKE
STORMY
BLACK HOLE OF DOOM

We spend the morning studying the water cycle, and I can't help but think of **NEPTUNE** where quite possibly the most expensive rain in the solar system falls—diamond hailstones. Amazingly I manage to stay on task. Good job, because I need to see Jess—she's been avoiding me all morning. I find her on the bench at breaktime, writing in a notepad.

'Sorry about yesterday.' I sit beside her. 'Brought you this to cheer you up. It's my favourite book.'

It's the first time I've ever lent anyone my **1001 SPACE FACTS**. And only because I'm pretty certain Jess understands the concept of borrowing.

'Thanks, Stan. I'm sorry too.' She hands me her notepad on which she's drawn a complicated diagram. 'I've tried my best at finding our common multiples, but it's taken me at least two hours and a headache to come up with this . . .'

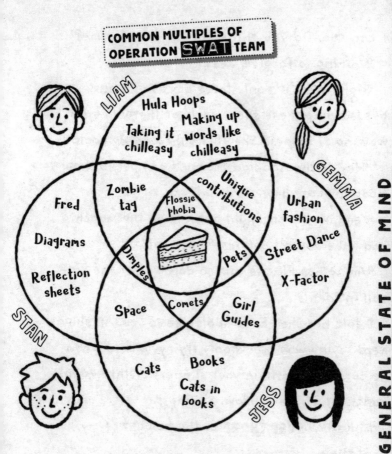

COMMON MULTIPLES OF OPERATION **SWAT** TEAM

LIAM

Hula Hoops

Taking it chilleasy

Making up words like chilleasy

GEMMA

Zombie tag

Unique contributions

Fred

Flossie phobia

Urban fashion

Diagrams

Dimples

Pets

Street Dance

Reflection sheets

X-Factor

STAN

Space

Comets

Girl Guides

Cats

Books

Cats in books

JESS

'Impressive. Although basically it just comes down to cake, then?' I roll my eyes.

'Well, we do share 99.9% DNA. And I THINK we all want to win. But not without a lot of compromise. Which is part of being a team, I guess. So . . . if you can work with Gemma and Liam, then

I can too. Do you think they'll forgive me?'

'Nothing to forgive, Jess.'

'Right. Well, it's only three days so I'd best get learning these space facts or there'll be no wowing of judges.' She flicks through my book.

'Hey, if the Apollo astronauts can get to the moon in three days . . .'

'Yeah, well Liam might get left on the launch pad if he doesn't pull his finger out.'

'Um, so has Flossie calmed down after the golf ball incident?'

'I told her she has to apologize to you. All she kept saying was Fred's only trying to help when he puts toothpaste in your slippers or throws your pants out of the window. Siblings!'

I blush a **LEVEL THREE** at the thought of my pants being discussed.

'Plus I've got to give up two months' worth of pocket money to help pay for the damage because *YOU SHOULD KNOW BETTER THAN TO GIVE FLOSSIE ACCESS TO GOLF BALLS*.' She stands up as the bell rings. 'Final SWAT session after school on Friday?'

'Believe me, I'll be there.'

Because I've never been so close to owning a telescope.

'I love Wednesdays!' Fred giggles as he skips towards Gran's for our weekly dose of cake. There's no need of a scarf now I've got Gran's trick up my sleeve. I catch him up at the grass verge counting buttercups.

'So how did the solar eclipse lesson go?'

'Flossie ate the orange they were using for the sun. Good job I brung another.'

'Wasn't it amazing how the moon and sun exactly match up even though—'

'I yawned a bit. Why's there so much pencil stuff at school?'

'But isn't it phenomenal how the sun—'

'Is Flossie a human?'

I sigh, realizing this isn't going to be a lovely bonding moment about space. And unfortunately I haven't packed my noise-can-

OVER THE MOON

SUNNY

CALM

OK

PHEW

NOT OK

ALARMED

NEED CAKE

STORMY

BLACK HOLE OF DOOM

MY GENERAL STATE OF MIND

celling headphones, so I can't avoid the following onslaught of questions:

WOULD MY TUMMY REALLY POP?

HOW ARE EYES MADE?

WHAT DOES THE QUEEN DO APART FROM WAVE AND WEAR A LEMON DRESS?

WHEN CAN I HAVE AN ELEPHANT?

DID THEY NOT HAVE PANTS IN THE GREEK AGES?

ARE WE REALLY ONE HUNDRED PER CENT UGLY INSIDE?

HOW D'YOU SAY BONJOUR IN FRENCH?

Thankfully Gran's house is only eight questions away.

SUNNY
CALM
OK
PHEW
NOT OK
ALARMED
NEED CAKE
STORMY
BLACK HOLE of DOOM

MY GENERAL STATE OF MIND

'You can't make a cake without licking the spoon!' she announces, greeting us at the door with two wooden spoons smothered in cake mix.

'Thanks, Gran!' We grab one each.

'You saved that dinosaur yet?' she says, and I notice she's added glitter to her blue highlights today—her hair resembles a nebula packed with fledgling stars.

'Um . . . no . . .' I look across at Fred, hoping he won't burst into tears. 'We're sort of . . . banned from the museum.'

'What a to-do!' she whistles, placing a plate of brownies in front of us. 'You need a wily plan. You're Foxes aren't you? I was one of eight—un-believable I know—but when we got banned from the zoo because our Cyril hugged a peacock, I volunteered for a week shovelling camel poo. So what's the plan to get yourselves un-banned?'

'I can cry out of my eyes,' Fred says, believing this is a valid contribution.

'Fair dos when the time comes Freddie, but you might need a bit more than that up your sleeve. You can't wait for things to happen, you

have to go out and make them happen,' Gran says,
popping a bobble-hat on his head. 'So get noshing.
I've organized a little trip out this evening!'

I wasn't expecting to be stood in a wooded glade
behind the museum. Gran usually takes us to bingo.

'Good evening everyone,' says Mr Hadfield.
'Welcome to Camford Museum's Dusk Walk. A
chance to spot some local wildlife.'

'Will we see lions?' Fred gasps.

'No,' he replies, handing out night-vision
binoculars. 'And it's important we keep to the path.'

'Cos of the lions?' Fred gasps again.

'There are NO lions. And the quieter we are, the
better.'

Fred tries to keep up with Mr Hadfield so he
can ask a million questions.

What kind of
poo is that? he asks, pointing his
binoculars to the path.

The only lion round here is in the sky as
I spot the constellation of Leo through my
binoculars. I'm amazed by the amount of stars
I can see away from the street lamps.

'OK, gather round,' Mr Hadfield whispers.
'Much of the bracken here is thick enough
to give cover to fox and deer. We'll take a
moment to observe.'

It's definitely given cover to one fox. My

OVER THE MOON

SUNNY

CALM

OK

PHEW

NOT OK

ALARMED

NEED CAKE

STORMY

BLACK HOLE of DOOM

MY GENERAL STATE OF MIND

night vision binoculars pick out Fred hiding behind a bush.

'RAHHHH!'
he yells, leaping out at me and frightening away our chances of seeing anything at all.

'SSSHHH!'
shushes everyone else.

'Righto, let's move along. Hopefully there's a chance of spotting something in the clearing. *IF* we're quiet.' Mr Hadfield pats Fred's head. Luckily his hat keeps in the wet donkey smell.

'Didn't fink I'd see you none more,' Fred sniffs, taking hold of Mr Hadfield's jacket sleeve.

'I'm sorry you were banned,' he says, shining his torch ahead. 'There wasn't much damage to Earth that couldn't be fixed with a bit of spit and polish.'

'I'm missing Rory. Can you sneak me in before he goes away in the cupboard?'

'Unfortunately there's CCTV everywhere, so I

might lose my job if I did that. OK, folks, if you train your binoculars into the long grass, you'll definitely spot something.'

Rabbits, dozens of them, sat frozen, their eyes glinting like tiny stars.

'Can I borrow your radio?' Fred shouts, pulling it from Mr Hadfield's belt and jumping up and down on a log. 'Charlie, Tango, Teacup, Johnny, Freddie Fox jumping in the woods, over!'

'REX WATCH? IS THAT YOU?' it crackles back. 'ARE YOU IN NEED OF BACK UP, WILCO AND OUT?'

'Here! That's museum property!' Mr Hadfield grabs it out of his hands. 'All fine here Mary, ahem, Eagle Eyes, false alarm. Roger and out.'

The rabbits have hopped it with all the commotion.

'Did you used to like dinosaurs?' Fred asks, jumping on a tree stump and leaning on Mr Hadfield's arm, oblivious to personal space barriers.

'We can't be into dinosaurs for ever,' he

whispers. 'As my mother used to say, got to move on, grow up, get an interest in something that's still alive!'

'You CAN love dinosaurs for ever,' Fred says. 'Rory had teeth the size of narnas during the upper wotsit thingy, a theropod up to loads of metres long, weighing more than a lot, becoming dead approximately sixty-five gajillion—'

'Well I'll be!' exclaims Mr Hadfield turning to look at him. 'You remembered?'

'You're an expert,' Gran pipes up. 'He learnt from the best.'

'Maybe. But in Mr Banner's museum I'm an old fossil too. Right, this way, look out for bats!'

'Does Mr Banner not love dinosaurs?' Fred asks, running beside him.

'He likes looking forward towards the future. And the future is all about upcycling. Which is why Rory and I will be retiring together.'

'You can't do that!' I gasp a bit too loudly. 'Fred won't have anyone to answer his questions.'

Apart from me, which is why I gasped at full volume.

'Perhaps he needs reminding that us fossils aren't over the hill.' Gran nudges him. 'You're a gem, Mr Hadfield. What you need is upcycling too. Look at what you taught my Fred.'

'Oh, well, um, very kind of you to say,' he nods towards Gran.

'You just need to teach that Mr Banner a thing or two as well. And while you're at it, tell him to un-ban my grandsons, or he'll have a protest on his hands. I'm a force of nature, Mr Hadfield. The centre of the hurricane may be calm, but you wouldn't want to cross me.'

Her icy stare makes him gulp. 'I don't doubt that, madam. If I could do anything about the ban, I would, you know.'

Our walk is over. We hand in our night vision binoculars, as Gran hands over a parcel of brownies.

'Oh, very kind, but no need, Mrs, um—'

'Trixie, single, dab hand at salsa if you own a pair of Cuban heels. And I meant what I said. You're a gem, Mr Hadfield. So are my grandsons. Mr Banner just needs to realize it.'

MY GENERAL STATE OF MIND

OVER THE MOON
SUNNY
CALM
OK
PHEW
NOT OK
ALARMED
NEED CAKE
STORMY
BLACK HOLE of DOOM

It's now become very clear why Gran has dragged us on this walk. To scare the living daylights out of Mr Hadfield with a menace sandwich—mild threat served between two slices of charm. Gran's speciality. And it nearly always works.

As the group disperses there are mutterings of 'FRIGHTENED ALL THE RABBITS', 'LIONS INDEED', 'NO IDEA ABOUT PERSONAL SPACE', and suddenly I feel quite protective. Fred may be a pain, but he's MY pain. Quite frankly it's difficult to control inappropriate bruv volume when you didn't know you were going on a nature walk (and you don't own a **NIGHT-OUT-WITH-A-BRUV-IN-THE-WOODS KIT** anyway).

TURN SIDEWAYS FOR MY
AMAZING PIE CHART

PERCENTAGE OF INAPPROPRIATE
BRUV VOLUME EXPECTED OVER A YEAR

Shouting 'I Don't' at the exact wrong moment during a wedding ceremony

Reciting everyone's lines as well as his own at the school nativity

Endless chatter on an unexpected woodland walk

Running commentary on which lady has the biggest bottom in Mum's yoga class

Burping the alphabet during the school prayer

Suspicious rah-ing in the dinosaur section of the library

Harmonica accompaniment during Gran's bingo

My stargazing accompanied by The Fart Symphony in D Major

⌐⇒BRUV BINGO

The universe has a diameter of about ninety-three billion light years. And that's just the bit we can see. The size of the whole universe could go on for ever and ever. A bit like the journey to school with Fred.

'I'm a bit sit-downy.'

'You MUST keep walking, Fred, or we'll be late.' Mum is dragging him along by the scarf.

Our journey should be fifteen minutes tops, but takes an hour. I know, I've worked it out:

FRED'S SCHOOL ROUTE TIMETABLE	PUDDLE	SNAIL	EMPTY CRISP PACKET	STICK	PEBBLE	SLUG
Front Door	8.15	8.16	8.20	8.23	8.24	8.32

'I'm going as quickly enough as I can, you moo-bag.'

'Frederick Fox!' she shouts. 'Don't you dare use that language with me!'

'I don't need this none more.' He pulls on the scarf. 'Make me run and count stuff like Gran does!'

'Gran always THINKS she knows best, but remind me what happened to Earth when she was in charge?' Mum says, mopping her brow as we finally reach the school gates. 'Now, I need you home promptly today.'

'I can't! It's our last SWAT team-up before the science fair.'

'I can't neither,' Fred says. 'I got snails to look at.'

GRAN'S GARDEN GATE	BUTTERCUP	CAT	FLOSSIE'S SKIP	CORNER SHOP	SCHOOL
8.40	8.46	8.51	8.55	9.06	9.15

MY GENERAL STATE OF MIND

OVER THE MOON · SUNNY · CALM · OK · PHEW · NOT OK · ALARMED · NEED CAKE · STORMY · BLACK HOLE OF DOOM

'Science and snails are *NOT* the centre of the universe.'

'That's where you're wrong because there *IS* no centre to the universe—it's continually expanding, which is hard to get your head round, I'll admit, but—'

'I'll be the judge of that!' Mum interrupts. 'Please get home on time—it's Gran's birthday, I've booked Gino's and I've baked a cake!'

'Yes Mum!' we both say together, standing upright like soldiers.

Luckily Jess is happy to switch our meeting to lunchtime: 'Well it *IS* your Gran's birthday.'

All I need to do now is make sure I don't get another reflection sheet.

'Eyes wide Year Six! Today we're doing science!' Mr Fisher yells as he enters the classroom.

Everyone groans. Except me. Because he's just pinned the periodic table of elements on the wall.

'Anyone ever heard the phrase *WE ARE ALL MADE OF STARDUST?*'

Obviously I put my hand up.

'A romantic notion, but a true one,' Mr Fisher says, pointing to the poster. 'These elements are the building blocks of life. And the ninety-two natural elements that make up everything on this planet were created at the heart of a star. Including you, Liam Miller, please stop eating!'

'Um, sir?' Liam says, scrunching up his crisp packet. 'Were even Hula Hoops created from a star?'

'Potatoes are a carbohydrate, which is carbon, hydrogen, and oxygen.' He points to them on the table. 'So yes, even Hula Hoops.'

'And jam?'

'Yes.'

'And pyjamas? And fleas? And eyebrows?'

Liam's never been so interested in science.

'Can we just get on, Year Six?' he snaps, handing out templates. 'I'd like you to fill in a table. And NO talking.'

The temptation to draw one up for Fred is just too great:

OVER THE MOON

SUNNY

CALM

OK

PHEW

NOT OK

ALARMED

NEED CAKE

STORMY

BLACK HOLE OF DOOM

MY GENERAL STATE OF MIND

NOT-NOBLE GASES		COMMON DEPOSITS			DODGY PARTICLES	
Rf RADIO-ACTIVE FART	**Db** DINNER BURP				**Ft** FLUFFY TOY	**Cr** CRISPS & RICE
Lt LOUD TRUMP	**Sbd** SILENT BUT DEADLY	**Bg** BOGEY	**Tc** TOAST CRUMBS	**Dr** DRIBBLE	**Us** UNDER-BED SNAIL	**Rb** REGURG-ITATED BROCCOLI
Ab AFTER-NOON BELCH	**Sf** STINKY FEET	**Ni** NITS	**Sd** SNEEZE DEBRIS	**Ge** GRASSY ELBOW	**Lv** LAV-LAV SNAKE	**Cy** CRAYON
Nw NOXIOUS WIND	**Mb** MORNING BREATH	**Mk** MUDDY KNEES	**A** ANNOY-INGNESS	**Wd** WET DONKEY	**Ubs** UNDER-BED SHARK	**Tw** TWO BY TWO

'Tell me, Mr Fox, I appear to have forgotten,' Mr Fisher angrily whispers over my shoulder. 'Is a radioactive fart a noble gas?'

BELIEVE ME, MR FISHER, I want to say, THERE'S NOTHING NOBLE ABOUT FRED'S RADIOACTIVE FARTS. WHICH IS WHY I'VE CLEARLY PUT THEM IN THE NOT-NOBLE GASES COLUMN.

'Shall I go grab a reflection sheet?' I offer.

'Oh yes, Mr Fox, oh yes indeed.'

Which means multi-tasking at lunchtime with an exasperated Jess, who's partly exasperated because I can't multi-task, but mainly because Gemma has just handed out the costumes.

'I'll do the comet tail, even glitter,' sighs Jess, 'but there's no way I'm wearing harem dance trousers. Comets don't wear harem dance trousers.'

'They don't wear bandanas either,' I say, as Gemma ties a starry-patterned one on my head with loads of ribbons stapled to it.

'Stanley, you're a MODERN-DAY COMET. You need swagger. Think science fused with rap.'

Think science fused with I'm completely out of my comfort zone.

'Seriously guys,' Jess says, colouring in an excellent drawing of the Arizona crater. 'The science fair is TOMORROW, and we've still got all these facts to learn. And we need a proper team name, and a velvet pedestal for the meteorite. And quite possibly a replacement for

MY GENERAL STATE OF MIND

OVER THE MOON

SUNNY

CALM

OK

PHEW

NOT OK

ALARMED

NEED CAKE

STORMY

BLACK HOLE OF DOOM

Liam seeing as he's not shown up. Even though I've baked double-chocolate muffins.'

Mrs Parker knocks on the door, interrupting once again.

'Sorry to disturb. Ooh, nice bandana, Stanley.'

I quickly take it off. 'Is it Freddie again?'

'Science fair. Mrs Riley's asked for an update.' She helps herself to a muffin. 'Are you all ready?'

'SOME of us are, Mrs Parker.' Jess looks up from her poster.

'Where's Liam?'

'Right behind you, miss!' He's stood there stroking a cushion. 'It's velvet, see? Borrowed it from the library. Plus I've learnt a fact: SPACE IS COMPLETELY ENORMOUS. And come up with a team name—CRATERMATES. Thank me later, guy-bros!'

'Um . . .' and then I realize I don't want to deflate this rare display of enthusiasm for something that's not Hula Hoops. 'That's great, Liam.'

'Ok, listen up CraterMates.' Mrs Parker sits on the table. 'Larkfield Primary are entering too. You

know what our history is with THAT school.
Mrs Riley's keen for a win, after losing Battle
of the Choirs last year.'

'We'll boosh it, miss, no worries.'

'I hope so, Liam, I really do. Just don't let me
down. I've put my neck on the line for this.'

'You'll lose your job?' Jess gasps.

'Of course not. I've just always wanted to say
that. Oh, and this is for Fred.' She hands me a
leaflet. 'Thought it best to give it to you. Most
of his letters home turn into aeroplanes and
end up in the bush by the bike shed.'

I look down at the leaflet. It's covered in
pictures of Rory, and one of Mr Noke, stood
on the lawn with his clipboard and megaphone.
*COME AND SHOW YOUR SUPPORT FOR
RORY!* It's a last-ditch attempt to protest
before the museum shuts for refurbishment.
And when's the protest? Tomorrow. The same
day as Operation SWAT.

MY GENERAL STATE OF MIND

OVER THE MOON

SUNNY

CALM

OK

PHEW

NOT OK

ALARMED

NEED CAKE

STORMY

BLACK HOLE of DOOM

'You don't have to take me anywhere fancy. I just need a fruit-based cocktail and Tony the salsa instructor,' Gran protests as we lead her into the restaurant.

I'm not sure Gino's is fancy, unless you count the stuck-up waiters, and the fish tank in the window.

'I've made you a fun birthday activity, Gran!'

'Ooh, smashing, Stanley!'

My younger brother was not made for restaurants where you need the ability to sit on a chair and eat. Which makes for an ideal game of:

➡ BRUV BINGO ⬅

SPILLS DRINK ON STANLEY	STANDS ON CHAIR AND LOUDLY ANNOUNCES SOMETHING	ASKS THE WAITER FOR CRISPS AND RICE	USES CUTLERY FOR EVERYTHING BUT PURPOSE IT WAS INVENTED FOR
FAKE CRIES BECAUSE HE HAS TO EAT PEAS	FLICKS CONDIMENTS OVER FAMILY MEMBERS	HAS TO BE TAKEN TO THE FISH TANK TO KILL TIME	SNEEZES IN STANLEY'S PUDDING

Make your own—it'll just about take the
sting out of the embarrassment.

'Crisps and rice!' demands Fred, using
the cutlery to brush his hair as the waiter
hovers over us.

'I'm afraid that is not on the menu,' he
answers sternly.

'Could we have the salmon fillet on a bed of
rice . . .' Dad sighs, 'but without the salmon?'

'JUST a bed of rice?' the waiter questions
with an expression of WHAT SPECIES OF
HUMAN AM I DEALING WITH HERE?

'Yes. And at half the price if possible.'

When it arrives, Mum sprinkles over the
prawn cocktail crisps she's stashed in her
bag (we've always got loads—nobody else can
stand them).

'Extra more!' Fred demands, standing on
his chair.

'That's enough crisps!' Dad whisper-shouts,
smothering his pizza in brown sauce. 'Now sit
down!'

'Blimey, I only need one more for a line!'

MY GENERAL STATE OF MIND

OVER THE MOON
SUNNY
CALM
OK
PHEW
NOT OK
ALARMED
NEED CAKE
STORMY
BLACK HOLE OF DOOM

laughs Gran, excitedly waiting for the moment Fred spills a drink on me.

He obliges, ten seconds after the waiter delivers our cokes. Obviously I anticipated this and wore my waterproof trousers—bit warm on a sunny day but they've already paid off.

I decide it's time to bring up the Rory protest and hand Mum the leaflet.

'Any chance you can take him? Only it's tomorrow, the same day as the science fair.'

'But he's banned from the museum, dimple-pops,' Mum says. 'And quite frankly I don't fancy another visit from the Earth police.'

'It won't be *INSIDE* the museum, Mum.'

'So it'll be standing around in the actual outside? With no chance of a cappuccino?'

'What about Dad then?'

'He's helping decorate my living room!' Gran says, slurping her strawberry mojito. 'I'm having polka-dots everywhere. You won't catch me with magnolia walls—that way leads the path to lace doilies and Aled Jones.'

'I can go all by myself,' Fred proclaims. 'I know

the way.'

'Of course you don't!' Mum tuts.

'Will *YOU* take me Stanley?' he looks at me
with a wobble in his lip.

'I wish I could, but it's <u>OPERATION SWAT</u>.
I've been planning it for ages and I can't let
my team down,' I feel awful as soon as I say it.
'Sorry Fred . . .'

'All right,' Mum sighs. 'At least I can keep
him away from anything expensive.'

'Thanks, Mum,' I say, as Fred sprinkles
pepper on his spoon and starts flicking it at
everyone.

'I want pudding!' he shouts.

'Not until you've eaten some of my peas,'
Mum says, scraping them on to his plate. 'You
have to eat at least one vegetable this week.'

'I'm not eating that scusting stuff, they look
like bogies.'

'You don't normally have a problem eating
them,' Dad says, as Fred starts to fake cry, so
Mum quickly drags him to look at the fish tank
in the window.

MY GENERAL STATE OF MIND

OVER THE MOON
SUNNY
CALM
OK
PHEW
NOT OK
ALARMED
NEED CAKE
STORMY
BLACK HOLE OF DOOM

'I only need one more for a full house!' Gran chuckles as she crosses off another square.

To sneeze in my pudding. It's inevitable. As the waiter brings out the birthday cake the whole restaurant sings 'Happy Birthday'. Fred rushes back to help Gran blow out the candles but instead sneezes over EVERYONE'S pudding.

yells Gran.

'Oh Frederick!' Mum moans. 'That took me all day!'

'No harm done.' Gran dabs at it with her napkin then serves up hefty slices.

I reluctantly put a piece on my spoon.

'There's no beetroot in it, Stanley.' Mum looks at me sternly.

I put it in my mouth, then immediately spit it out, along with everyone else.

'What DID you put in it then?' Dad cries, wiping his tongue on a napkin and gulping water.

'The usual . . . flour, eggs, sugar—'

'And special sauce!' Fred pipes up, the only one still eating it.

'What special sauce?' Mum frowns.

'The chocolate sauce Daddy has on his food,' Fred says proudly. 'I squeezed loads in as a surprise.'

RECIPE FOR DISASTER
* 1 Bruv
* 1 Abandoned cake mix
* 1 Bottle of brown sauce
Mix for yuck!

'Oh good grief,' Mum shakes her head. 'When will I learn not to leave the mixing bowl alone? I've baked a brown sauce cake . . .'

At least I've got a new one for the bingo card.

☆

'The stars are in the sky and the moon is spankaling.' Fred yawns as I give him a piggy back to look out of the window.

The moon is slowly moving away from EARTH. Fred's the opposite: orbiting around my personal space like a buzzy satellite.

MY GENERAL STATE OF MIND

OVER THE MOON

SUNNY

CALM

OK

PHEW

NOT OK

ALARMED

NEED CAKE

STORMY

BLACK HOLE OF DOOM

'Wos that?' he points.

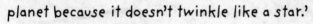'VENUS. You can tell it's a planet because it doesn't twinkle like a star.'

'Do people live there?'

'They'd be spinning backwards if they did. And apart from the toxic atmosphere and the sulphuric acid rain, I'm sure it'd be a smashing place to live.'

'Look!' he gasps. 'A shooty star!'

'I think that's a helicopter.'

'Can I still make a wish?'

'Course.' I put him down and grab the perspex box. 'Cos I've got a shooting star right here.'

'It's a rock . . .' He looks angry-puzzled.

'Yeah, but it's a space rock. Cool, eh?' I let him hold it.

'You LOVE space, don't you, Stan?'

'About as much as you love dinosaurs.'

'That must be a massive lot.'

He grips the rock tightly, screws up his face, and holds his breath for a few seconds. 'Finished wishing!' he blurts out. 'Can I have it under my pillow now? Then it really will come true.'

'How does that work?'

'It's magic, that's why the tooth fairies come. And the bogey fairies.'

'The *BOGEY* fairies . . .?' I stare at his grubby little face, with his big pleading eyes, and against my better judgement, wrap it in one of my socks and place it under his pillow. 'Time for bed.'

'But I'm not tired,' he yawns.

I kiss his ear—the one part of his face that's clean. 'Night, night, Fred. Get a good sleep, we've got a big day tomorrow.'

By the time I climb into bed, he's snoring like an ogre.

OVER THE MOON

SUNNY

CALM

OK

PHEW

NOT OK

ALARMED

NEED CAKE

STORMY

BLACK HOLE OF DOOM

MY GENERAL STATE OF MIND

⮕ FLIBBING

'Wakey, wakey, nice and shiny!' Fred shouts in my ear, and then he sneezes all over my face.

Thank goodness we're not on board <u>THE INTERNATIONAL SPACE STATION</u>—with sixteen sunrises every day, he'd have far too many opportunities to sneeze on me.

I scoff down breakfast, grab my rucksack and cardboard box of equipment.

Before I leave I have to help Fred into his dinosaur costume. No matter how much I try to quicken the process, it's not helped by the fact he forgets to bend his limbs. It's like dressing a tree.

'All done,' I say, wiping my brow after half an hour of struggling.

'I need a wee,' comes a muffled cry from beneath the dinosaur head.

Just brilliant. Ages later and I've got him

OVER THE MOON

SUNNY

CALM

OK

PHEW

NOT OK

ALARMED

NEED CAKE

STORMY

BLACK HOLE of DOOM

MY GENERAL STATE OF MIND

dressed again.

'I got tummyflies. I've forgot how to play the harmonica . . .'

He's never known how to play the harmonica, let's be honest.

'You're just nervous, Fred,' I say, helping him into his gigantic dinosaur slippers. 'I've got tummyflies too. Good luck saving Rory.'

'Good luck in space, Stan.'

'If you need me, call my mobile,' says Dad, dropping me off at the town hall car park.

As I'm walking up the steps, Liam pulls up on his bike with a rucksack full of Hula Hoops.

'Can always rely on you to remember a multipack.'

'Hey, is the moon round, dude-bro?' He high fives me.

'I think you'll find it's egg-shaped.' Jess takes the words out of my mouth as we walk in on her setting up display boards, on the back of which she's pinned paper to occupy Flossie and her crayons. 'Um, Floss, is there something you need to say to Stan?'

She snarls at me. 'Sorry I bashed your legs as hard as I completely could, and tried to knock your head off with a golf ball. Now you should say sorry to Fred.'

She runs off, jabbing a foam cutlass at anyone who walks by, including Gemma who has just arrived with her props box and a face covered in glitter.

"S'up comets!" She hands out our tinselled bandanas and tails. 'Ready to wipe out those judges?'

'Ready to look stupiculous,' Liam mumbles, as Gemma sticks stars on his face.

I note no one else has costumes as I check out the competition: there's an exhibit on solar eclipses with a projection on a bed sheet; a display claiming PLUTO is still a planet (they have my sympathy); and in the corner with a lot of glitter and star signs are Team Astro, who will 'READ YOUR PERSONALITY, YOUR DESIRES, YOUR FUTURE, USING THE ANCIENT ART OF ASTROLOGY'.

'How did they even get in?' tuts Jess.

'I know, right. That's just NOT science.'

Although it does get me thinking. If planets had personalities I know which one Fred would be:

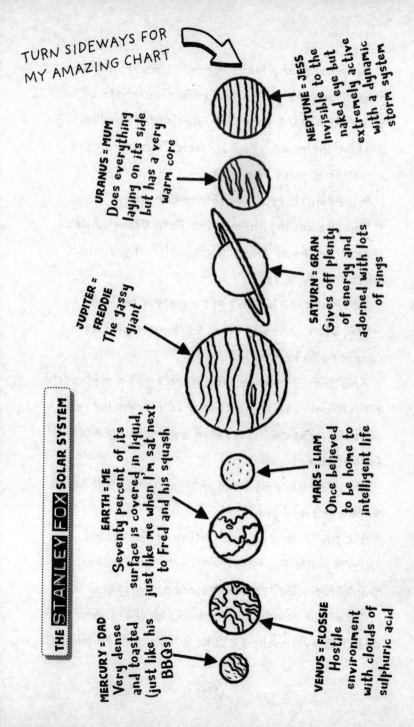

But what really takes my eye is an exhibit about gravity and weight, with a blown-up photo of BUZZ ALDRIN'S famous footprint left in the dust on the moon. It's Larkfield Primary, already strutting around like winners.

'Nice tail!' they shout out, snickering.

'They're calling themselves Zero Gravity.' Jess shakes her head. 'There's no such thing. I mean, microgravity, sure.'

'At least they haven't got a meteorite.'

'Um, Stan . . .' calls Liam. 'Is the perspex box supposed to be empty?'

And then I realize we haven't got a meteorite either, because it's at home underneath Fred's pillow. I was so distracted by dressing Fred I forgot to fetch it.

'Oh no!' I sink my head into my hands. 'I'll have to go back and get it.'

'No time!' Jess says, pointing at the crowd filtering into the hall, along with four judges. 'Don't worry. At least we're not astrologers.'

True. Our crater display looks brilliant. And Jess has even baked a cake with a sunken middle.

'I had to open the oven door just at the right moment to achieve that.'

But none of it detracts from the

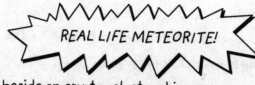

REAL LIFE METEORITE!

sign beside an empty velvet cushion.

'Leave it with me, space-bros,' Liam says, dashing outside, his comet tail flickering after him.

I've seen Liam's ideas before, including his Savoury Stationery (threading pens with Hula Hoops so you can snack while you write), so I'm not holding my breath. He appears holding his T-shirt up to his stomach, packed full of pebbles.

'Got them from the car park. Wasn't sure what looked more like a space rock.'

'That would be none of them.' I roll my eyes, fishing out a dark stone. 'This will have to do.'

Luckily my mind is taken off the dodgy meteorite by a family who want to do our experiment.

'I want to make loads of craters!' says a boy not much older than Fred, so I steady the

OVER THE MOON

SUNNY

CALM

OK

PHEW

NOT OK

ALARMED

NEED CAKE

STORMY

BLACK HOLE OF DOOM

MY GENERAL STATE OF MIND

steps as he drops oranges, marbles, and golf balls into the bowls of sand. Jess has put a layer of powdered blue paint on top so the craters look even better.

There's even a small queue of people by the time a judge wanders along.

'I understand you have a meteorite?' he says, putting on his glasses. 'Is this it?'

'Um . . . yes . . .' A blush travels over my face.

'A meteoroid, captured by Earth's gravitational force, can accelerate up to seventy kilometres per second,' Jess recites. 'Once it enters our atmosphere, it flashes brightly as a meteor, or shooting star. And if it hits Earth it becomes a meteorite. Most actually vaporize before they hit the ground. But not this one.'

No. Not this one. This is a pebble from the car park that has never accelerated anywhere.

'Hmmm . . .' he studies it closely and makes a note on his clipboard.

'Most meteorites come from asteroids,' Jess starts up again. 'But some come from the moon.'

'I see . . .' says the judge who starts to wander

off towards Zero Gravity.

'Which is exactly where this one comes from—*THE MOON*,' she blurts out.

'Really?' he stops in his tracks. 'Interesting ... I'm guessing it's been officially recognized by the Meteoritical Society? And that you're claiming to possess a <u>VERY RARE</u> meteorite?'

'Um ... yep,' Jess squeaks, flushing fiery crimson.

Fortunately he's called away by another judge to Larkfield's display.

'Why did you say all that?' I whisper. 'Especially when it's a pebble from the car park!'

'I thought you were brillendous,' nods Liam. 'So, is it, like, *REALLY* from the moon?'

'Obviously not, cos you just got it from the car park!' Jess hisses at him.

'Well let's hope the judge doesn't know that, or we're in trouble for fibbing.'

'It's not fibbing, Stanley, it's ... flibbing.' Jess bites her lip. 'Ad-libbing and fibbing at the same time. He'd started to wander off to

No-Such-Thing-As-Zero-Gravity over there.'

It's not like I haven't heard a dodgy fib before. Fred does it all the time, although he always spills the beans when he tries to fib: '*I HONESTLY DIDN'T TAKE YOUR EAGLE MOON LANDER OFF THE SHELF AND HAXIDENTALLY LEAVE IT ON THE FLOOR SO IT HAXIDENTALLY GOT SQUISHED BY MY MUDDY SHOE.*'

'We've got work to do,' Jess reminds us, as she stops Flossie burying treasure in the sand.

I plot our results on a chart, and it reaches the same conclusion as the damage Fred's inflicted on my Death Star over the past few months: *LARGER METEORITES DROPPED FROM A GREATER HEIGHT CREATE THE BIGGEST CRATERS.*

'Good work CraterMates. Even Liam!' Mrs Parker has arrived, helping herself to a bag of crisps. 'So where's this famous meteorite?'

'Um . . .' I start to panic as Gemma nods frantically at me, turning her sequined baseball cap back to front, and I can't believe I'm about to say what I'm about to say. 'You're just in time for the Comet Swagger Rap, miss.'

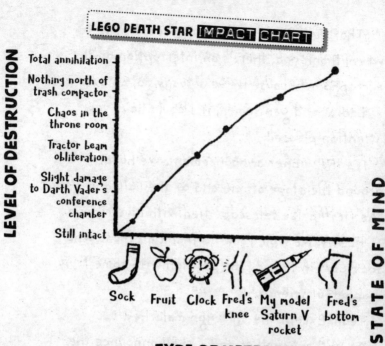

LEGO DEATH STAR IMPACT CHART

LEVEL OF DESTRUCTION

- Total annihilation
- Nothing north of trash compactor
- Chaos in the throne room
- Tractor beam obliteration
- Slight damage to Darth Vader's conference chamber
- Still intact

Sock | Fruit | Clock | Fred's knee | My model Saturn V rocket | Fred's bottom

TYPE OF METEORITE

Gemma pop-and-locks across the room, and we take up our positions as she starts to rap:

'Take it from the top! I'm a two-tailed ice rock, amino acid building-block, fiery-plumed peacock . . .'

We make lame attempts at the robot dance behind her.

'I'm supercool methane, higher than a' airplane, crusty as quiche Lorraine—break it down!'

MY GENERAL STATE OF MIND

SUNNY | CALM | OK | PHEW | NOT OK | ALARMED | NEED CAKE | STORMY | BLACK HOLE OF DOOM

That's my cue to start urban freestyling,
when, thank god, there's an interruption on the
microphone because we've actually got an audience.

'Ladies and gentlemen, if I could have your
attention please!'

It's the winner announcement. We huddle
around the stage at one end of the hall, and I spot
the first-prize telescope tied with blue ribbon.

'Firstly, we would like to thank all those who
took part in today's competition with some truly
wonderful science.'

Yeah. Except the star sign malarkey.

'So without further ado, I shall announce the
winners in reverse order.' He clears his throat. 'In
third place . . . TEAM ASTRO!'

A polite round of applause. I can't believe
they've even placed.

'Second place goes to . . . SOLAR ECLIPSE
PROJECTION.'

They deserve it. The bed sheet projector was
inspired.

'And first place, a justifiable winner . . . superb
display . . . excellent experiment . . .'

He's obviously building it up like **X FACTOR**, and my heart's thumping.

'`ZERO GRAVITY` for their Weight on Other Worlds experiment! Well done Larkfield! Fascinating to find I'd be as light as a cat on `PLUTO`, heavy as an ostrich on `JUPITER`.'

A cheer goes up as my heart sinks. Not just because we didn't even place. But because even Liam has worked out the truth of their lame experiment.

'You'd die before you even had a chance to step on the scales, dude-bro! No airmosphere!' he says, shaking his head in disgust. 'AND your eyeballs would fall out, right, Stan?'

'Um, well—'

'AND you couldn't even put the scales down because `JUPITER` HAS NO SURFACE!' Jess hisses.

The judge comes back on the microphone. 'Unfortunately, I have some bad news for one team.'

'Oh flip. He's found us out.' Jess is now gripping my arm, and I realize I'm part of this deception whether I like it or not.

MY GENERAL STATE OF MIND

OVER THE MOON

SUNNY

CALM

OK

PHEW

NOT OK

ALARMED

NEED CAKE

STORMY

BLACK HOLE OF DOOM

'Regrettably we have to disqualify one of the schools that entered today.'

There's a gasp around the room. Mainly from Planet Pluto who are worried their protest hasn't gone down so well.

'I'm afraid that CRATERMATES are exempt from the certificate ceremony for trying to pass off a pebble as a rare meteorite. A meteorwrong if you will.'

'Hey that's us!' Liam actually waves, just to make sure EVERYONE in the room is now looking, as my face immediately glows red, along with Jess's, until we're roughly the same temperature as a hurtling meteor falling to Earth about to be engulfed by humiliation.

'How embarrassing,' grumbles Mrs Parker over the snickering coming from Larkfield. 'There'll be reflection sheets for this, and Stanley, a letter to your parents because you've just reached reflection sheet limit.'

'Shall we grab the Hula Hoops and leg it?' Liam already has them under his T-shirt.

'I'll take the blame,' Jess whispers to me. 'It's all my fault . . .'

'No. You did more than all of us put together. All I had to do was bring the meteorite and I couldn't even manage—'

WAIT MISTER!
WAIT!

A loud squeaky voice interrupts me. I spin around along with everyone else, to see a small dinosaur rushing into the hall, holding up a rock. He takes off his head (not his actual head, but the dinosaur costume head), and inside is a sweaty little brother. My sweaty little brother, bright red and panting, running as best he can in his gigantic dinosaur slippers up towards the judges.

'I got it! I got it!' he yells, shoving the rock into the hands of the judge and grabbing the microphone. 'I'm Fred! My ginormous bruvver forgot his shooty-star so I brung it to him.'

The judge wrestles the microphone away from him as Mum dashes into the hall, out of breath with her flip-flops under her arm.

'Mum!' I run over to her. 'What are you doing here?'

'Ran . . . all . . . the . . . way . . .' she puffs, holding her side. 'Need . . . lavender calming spray . . .'

'Oh . . . I see. . .' says the judge, turning the rock over in his hands and conferring with the others.

Fred tries to grab the mike back. 'Can I play my harmonica now?'

'Absolutely not! I have an announcement,' the judge says. 'A change to the results ladies and gentlemen, and dinosaurs . . . disqualification is lifted from CRATERMATES. Camford Primary can collect a certificate of participation after all!'

I know it's just a bit of paper, but I'll take that over disqualification and a letter home any day.

'Thank goodness!' Mrs Parker starts breathing again as we line up to collect our certificates.

'Sorry about that,' I say, shaking the judge's hand. 'And thanks for not disqualifying us.'

'Thank your brother. It was down to him. By the way,' he says, handing back my space rock. 'That's a stone meteorite you've got there. See those tiny grains? They contain minerals that are older than our planet, older than our solar system. We call them stardust.'

'Wow . . .' I say, studying it closely. 'That's amazing.'

'So make sure you look after it from now—oh!' the judge stops mid-sentence. 'My, how astonishing! You seem to have an asterism from the Ursa Major constellation upon your face!'

'Why yes I do . . .' I can't believe it. I've just shaken the hand of the first and probably last person who will ever correctly point that out. Judges at science fairs are obviously a better class of freckle-spotter, and know an asterism when they see one.

Mum kisses my cheek. 'Well done my little space-angel!'

'Thanks, Mum. But what about the protest?'

'Fred got so upset when he found the rock under his pillow. He said it was all his fault, and if we didn't bring it he'd start a brand new indoor snail collection. I've never run so fast.'

I look over at Fred, sat on the stage, swinging his legs, squeaking his harmonica.

OVER THE MOON

SUNNY

CALM

OK

MY GENERAL STATE OF MIND

PHEW

NOT OK

ALARMED

NEED CAKE

STORMY

BLACK HOLE OF DOOM

'Hey bruv.' I sit beside him and pop my bandana on his head. 'Can't believe you missed Rory for me.'

'I had to help my wish come true.'

'What wish?'

'That you win the space fair. You did win, didn't you?'

'Uh, yeah, course.' I hug him, spotting the telescope in the hands of Larkfield. 'Thanks for what you did for me.'

'He does stuff for you all the whole time,' Flossie says, swinging her cutlass dangerously close to my head.

'He does stuff TO me all the whole time. Like squeezing toothpaste in my slippers.'

'He's just trying to get them sparkily clean.'

'And putting ladybirds in my lunchbox?'

'So they eat all the lettuce you hate.'

'Licking all the crisps?'

'He's licking for prawn cocktail cos he knows you don't like them.'

'All right, explain chucking my pants out the window.'

'Trying to get rid of your manky space pants, didn't

you know?'

'Well, no.' I scratch my head. 'So you're telling me that *EVERY SINGLE TIME* he was just looking out for me?'

'Arrrh, Jim Lad.' She places the eyepatch back on her face.

'Right . . .' I frown. 'And cutting holes in my favourite T-shirt?'

'To let out the stinky armpit pong.'

Flossie's revelations have left me flummoxed.

'Aha! What about Wee Willie Winkie? Don't tell me *THAT'S* for my benefit!'

'Even *I* don't know why he does that. We all have our idiosyncrasies.'

I can't quite believe that all my brother's faffing about was done out of kindness. Or that a five-year-old girl has just said a word I don't understand.

I look up and see the picture of Buzz Aldrin's dusty boot print. I think of Fred jumping across the dinosaur footprints like stepping stones. And then I remember the museum banner:

Leave the right kind of footprint behind

And it hits me. Like a meteorite ready to wipe out the dinosaurs.

I switch on the mike. 'Can I have your attention please, um, everyone . . .'

Not surprisingly nobody looks up at me.

'Hey! Listen! I need to ask you all a BIG favour. And I can promise cake . . .'

NOW everyone's listening.

OVER THE MOON

SUNNY

CALM

OK

PHEW

NOT OK

ALARMED

NEED CAKE

STORMY

BLACK HOLE OF DOOM

MY GENERAL STATE OF MIND

↳TEAMWORK

SATURN'S rings are made up of pieces of ice and rock. Some are as small as a grain of sand, others as large as a mountain. And small shepherd moons orbit the gaps keeping the rings in place.

Flossie is a shepherd moon. Her hair has enough gravity to keep everyone in place.

SAVE THE RORY
YOU SCURVY DOGS!

she shouts, marching out in front, creating a gravitational pull, as we head down the street towards the museum.

Thanks to the power of cake, the teams from the science fair have joined us, even

ZERO GRAVITY, as Jess and I hold up the bed sheet kindly donated by **SOLAR ECLIPSE PROJECTION**, on brooms kindly donated by the town hall who don't realize they've donated them yet but we promise to return them later (because we understand the concept of borrowing).

'You do realize you've got nothing written on your banner.' Mr Noke scratches his forehead.

'Not yet we haven't,' I reply. 'How many signatures have you got?'

'Last count, um, eighty-four.'

'And kids still can't sign?'

'Against petition policy, I'm afraid.'

'Right. Over here everyone!'

I guide my mini army to the front lawn beside the dinosaur footprints just as Dad pulls up.

'Don't panic! The cake ambulance is here!' Gran gasps, climbing out the passenger side with a stack of tins.

Thank goodness they answered my emergency call. And that Gran can be relied upon to have cake for forty on hand at a moment's notice.

'Thanks Gran! And Dad, I need your dust sheets and spare paint.'

'Oh, OK son!' he grins, thinking this is a sign I'm keen to go into business with him.

'Jess—we need a bowl of soapy water; Mum—paint trays along here; Liam—help me spread out the bed sheet.'

'What are you up to, Stan?' Jess asks, having blagged a bucket of water from an ice-cream van.

'I'm completely winging it. Unusual for me, I know.'

I haven't even scribbled down a cake chart to help me work out the percentages of pulling this off. Before I know it, I'm pouring paint in the trays, and borrowing Mr Noke's megaphone. Not that Fred needs a megaphone, but we need everybody's attention in what little bit of afternoon we have left. While I prep my brother on what to say, Jess starts painting SAVE THE RORY on the back of our science fair posters and Gran sets out cake on Dad's wallpaper-pasting table

'OK Freddie, have you got it?'

'I got it, Stan. Easy-peasy orange-squeezey. But I'm absolutely a bit nervous.'

OVER THE MOON

SUNNY

CALM

OK

PHEW

NOT OK

ALARMED

NEED CAKE

STORMY

BLACK HOLE of DOOM

MY GENERAL STATE OF MIND

'You'll be fine. I'm right here with you.' I pick him up, making sure we're in front of the museum banner.

He puts the megaphone up to his mouth and bellows:

MAKE YOUR FOOTPRINT
COUNT! SAVE THE RORY!

Once I get my hearing back, and we have an audience, I help Fred take off his dinosaur feet, place his tiny right foot into the paint, and carefully plant it on the sheet. Leaving the right footprint behind.

'This is brilliant, Stan!' Mum exclaims, taking off her flip-flops. 'Go Team Fox! See what happens when we put our heads together?'

'Nits usually.'

As people pass the museum, children pull their parents towards the paint. Before long there's a queue of them snaking across the front lawn, stood in bare feet, waiting to sign their own petition.

'This way!' Mum says, leading them over to Gran

where they can eat cake and have their feet washed.

'Sorry I flibbed,' says Jess, planting a footprint. 'But it comes in handy sometimes. I've called the local TV station and flibbed to them too. I've told them there's masses of people protesting with feet and they'd better get down here quick if they want to see history made.'

'You sure know how to flib,' I say, placing my own footprint next to my brother's. It's half the size of mine, just as Mars is half the size of Earth. I've always thought of him as a Martian.

Even Larkfield plant their footprints, and then some little kids run across it planting way too many, and then a dog, a bike, and a couple of skateboarders (who am I to argue with their visible teenage biceps?) Flossie decides to place her feet AND her hands on the sheet, and I'm fine with that too.

'All right, Stan?' She prods my arm, and I'm surprised to note I've been promoted from bilge rat to my actual name. 'I ain't wotching

MY GENERAL STATE OF MIND

SUNNY | CALM | OK | PHEW | NOT OK | ALARMED | NEED CAKE | STORMY | BLACK HOLE OF DOOM you none more.'

'You're not going to make me walk the plank?'

'Not today, me hearties.' She runs off, her mad candyfloss hair whipped by the breeze.

'You got off lightly,' Jess says. 'Just ask Maisie Watlington in Year One.'

'Almost being killed by a golf ball? Threatened with the black spot? The worst humiliation I've ever known? I'd hate to see what NOT getting off lightly means,' I tut.

'Wos going on, we were in the middle of rehearsals?' Orson has rocked up with his bandmates. 'Your text sounded urgent. Has Floss been looting again?'

'It's a protest,' Jess explains. 'And where there's a protest, there's a song, right?'

'For sure,' he nods, as they sit under a tree and start jamming on their guitars. 'SAVE THE RORY, HE'S LIKE YOU AND ME, EXCEPT HE'S NOT, COS HE'S A DINOSAUR . . .'

'Woah!' Liam squats down with the band. 'You proper LIKE dinosaurs?'

'Who wouldn't, man?'

'I gotta go, be back soon.' He jumps up, and cycles off on his bike.

Freddie's on the megaphone again:

SAVE THE RORY! COME AND SEE MY GINORMOUS BRUVVER! HE USED TO WEAR SPACE ROCKET PANTS!

I quickly grab it back just as the museum doors fling open. It's John Banner.

'I'm afraid you're going to have to move, you haven't got permission to be on the front lawn,' he yells, pointing at me. 'And you! You're banned!'

'Now you wait a minute!' Gran shakes a finger at him. 'These young whippersnappers are getting their voices heard by voting with their feet.'

'The Fox brothers are banned from—'

'They're not banned from being outside in the fresh air!' She picks up a slice of cake. 'Now think on, and have some lemon drizzle.' And she shoves it in his gob before he can complain again.

'Foo late, anyhaw,' he mumbles, heading back inside and closing the doors.

The sheet has filled up with a multitude of footprints, and we haul it up on the broom handles. Dad grabs another dust sheet and two more paint pots from the back of his van. 'That's the last of it, son.'

'We're running low on people too,' I sigh. 'If only we had a way of letting them know we're here . . .'

It's Idris. Marching down the path with a crowd of kids from school, holding up their right shoes as they turn on to the front lawn.

He greets me with a fist bump.

'Liam texted. Apparently Orson says dinosaurs are cool now. And I mean, would you rather be doing your homework on textiles in the fourteenth century, or hanging with your mates eating cake? No brainer.' He gestures to the mob behind him.

Before long we've filled up another sheet and hung it from a tree, as more people gather to see what's going on.

'Just in time, mate.' I pat Liam on the back, as he rolls up on his bike, pulling a load of bedding from his rucksack.

'Not sure what Mum's gonna say about nicking her king-size bed sheet though.'

'I could hazard a guess . . .'

And then he pulls out his old duvet cover. The one with the diplodocus on.

'I thought you were denying all knowledge of its existence?' I question.

'Hey, who doesn't like dinosaurs, man?' And he hangs it up near the jamming guitars.

'Had one myself,' nods Orson.

OVER THE MOON

SUNNY

CALM

OK

PHEW

NOT OK

ALARMED

NEED CAKE

STORMY

BLACK HOLE OF DOOM

MY GENERAL STATE OF MIND

Soon we're out of paint and improvise with muddy puddles, drawing round feet with biros, holding shoes in the air, or randomly hanging them from the tree. Someone's even got a sign saying

SAVE THE STUFFED BADGER

but unfortunately he's not going anywhere.

As evening draws in, people are sat around singing along with Orson's band, eating cake, and urban freestyling with Gemma. I realize I haven't even brought my **BEING-OUTSIDE-WITH-A-BRUV KIT** (a frisbee, a ball, and a stick if you're asking—hey, it works for dogs).

Jess hands me a plate of cake. 'You'll be needing some serious me-time now.'

'Mmm, def'ly.' I try to swallow.

'P'raps we could watch a meteor shower—the Perseids are coming up in the summer.'

It's the best offer I've ever had in my life, so

of course I choke on the cake and splutter it out on my T-shirt. Some even comes out of my nose. <u>LEVEL TWO</u>. If I lived on MARS I'd blend right in.

She hands me a tissue from up her sleeve: 'TV crew's here.'

'Are you the Fox brothers?' A lady in bright red lipstick and brandishing a microphone taps me on the shoulder. 'We're going live in about ten minutes.'

'On telly?' I gulp.

'You'll be fine,' she says, putting tiny microphones on our jumpers.

'I'm gonna be famous!' yells Fred, as Mum rushes in to brush our hair.

'Remember, fox cubs, be true to who you are, and always check your teeth before going on local television,' she winks, inspecting our mouths.

'Three ... two ... one ... ON AIR,' signals the cameraman as I quickly pull Fred's finger out of his nose.

'Yes, good evening,' the presenter addresses the camera. 'Here in Camford today

MY GENERAL STATE OF MIND

SUNNY

CALM

OK

PHEW

NOT OK

ALARMED

NEED CAKE

STORMY

BLACK HOLE OF DOOM

a pair of brothers have been campaigning to save a T-rex, and made a whole community vote with their feet.'

All I can see is the red light and all I can think about is everyone in the whole world watching me.

'Stanley, if I can come to you first, what is it about Rory that made you drive this campaign forward?'

'Um . . . well . . . I wanted to, um . . .' My face starts to flush. 'It's about . . . um . . .'

Everything I've ever known has just vacated my brain. Then I spot Mr Noke, stood there with his clipboard.

'I wanted to help my brother!' I suddenly remember. 'He's always loved Rory. There was a petition, but lots of us couldn't sign it, I mean Fred can't really write much yet . . .'

'I can write the word poo!' he protests.

'Fred! Sorry . . . so I thought we could show our support in a different way. Make our footprints count. Because everyone should get the chance to walk into that grand hall and see an enormous T-rex skeleton from sixty-five million years ago.'

I turn to look into the camera. 'He belongs in the museum.'

'The campaign has taken off with social media—hashtag footprint has got lots of support this afternoon. Was that down to you too?'

'Uh, that was down to me.' Idris pokes his head into view. 'Idris. Techno whizz-kid. Just how I roll.'

The cameraman pans to the right to cut him out of shot.

'Freddie, why is Rory so important to you?'

'Cos all his skin fell off.'

'And how many footprints have you collected this afternoon?'

'FIVE GAJILLION!' he yells.

'Could a campaign like this really make a difference?' The reporter turns to camera as it focuses in on her. 'Well, we also spoke to the museum—'

SAVE THE RORY!

Fred yells into his microphone.

MY GENERAL STATE OF MIND

OVER THE MOON

SUNNY

CALM

OK

PHEW

NOT OK

ALARMED

NEED CAKE

STORMY

BLACK HOLE OF DOOM

'—and they put out a statement this evening stating—'

> HE COMES ALIVE AT NIGHT!

'—having considered all the opinions—'

> HE'S MY BEST FRIEND IN ALL THE WORLD, APART FROM MY GINORMOUS BRUVVER!

'—they were still driving ahead with their new and, I quote, "pioneering exhibition which they were sure would win round public opinion once they opened". So it looks as though Rory's journey ends here. And now back to the studio for the weather with Adam Phillips—'

I TRIED TO COLOUR HIM IN!

Fred shouts as the mike is taken off his jumper.

'He didn't really! Just a joke!' I speak into my mike as the red light goes off.

The reporter rolls her eyes at the cameraman: 'They say never work with children . . . or dinosaurs . . .'

Luckily all the excitement of being on telly means Fred didn't hear the statement from the museum. And looking at his little excited face I can't break it to him right now. It seems our teamwork hasn't paid off. Rory has just become extinct all over again.

↳ LISTENING

'The dark's come out,' says Fred, pulling on his dinosaur pyjamas.

'Time for bed.' I draw the curtains.

'The lipstick lady said Rory's journey ends? Wos that mean?'

'Um . . .' I don't quite know how to tell him. 'Sorry, bruv. I tried my best. But the museum have decided there's no room left for him.'

Fred's bottom lip starts wobbling, as Mum sits down on the bed.

'No one could say we didn't try,' she says, wiping his tears with her thumbs. 'But we just have to accept his time is over. He'll be roaring about in the great dinosaur museum in the sky.'

'But Stan helped and everything!'

'I know, pipsqueak-moose. Shall I go and make us a hot chocolate?'

He nods. As Mum leaves the room, he kneels at my bed, placing his hands together.

'Darth Vader, Halloween my name, forgive us this day our daily bread, and forgive all those who Christmas against us, look after Rory, for I am a kingdom, for ever and never, Arrrrr-men.'

'Great prayer, bruv,' I smile, doing up his pyjama buttons. 'Sorry I couldn't save him.'

'I'm going to the lav-lav,' he says, putting on his gigantic dinosaur slippers and wrapping himself in his dressing gown.

'When you come back, how about a bit of TWO BY TWO?'

He shrugs and walks off.

I look up at the science fair certificate on my wall. If it wasn't for Fred, I'd have had a detention instead. And I realize I haven't given the telescope a second thought since it happened. I tidy up the pile of dinosaurs on his bed, pop away his socks, and start sketching a cake chart of things I can do with him to take his mind off Rory.

'Here we go.' Mum comes back in and places

MY GENERAL STATE OF MIND

OVER THE MOON
SUNNY
CALM
OK
PHEW
NOT OK
ALARMED
NEED CAKE
STORMY
BLACK HOLE OF DOOM

the cups down. 'Oh, where is he?'

'Loo.'

'But he never goes on his own . . .' Mum says. 'I'll just go check he's OK.'

'Maybe he's grown up a bit these past few days,' I say, but then spot a lollipop stuck to the wall that he's saving for later.

OH MY GOD! I hear Mum yell.

'What is it?' I run out to the landing, thinking it'll be something involving my toothbrush.

'He's gone!' She rushes downstairs to the open front door; the footstool has been dragged from the lounge to open it.

Dad flings open the kitchen door. 'What's all the commotion, I'm burning toast in here!'

In five seconds I've squeezed into my trainers, grabbed my coat, and rushed out into the front garden.

FRED! FRED! I call out.

Dad runs out into the street yelling too.

'Where is he?' There's panic in Mum's eyes. 'He doesn't know the way to anywhere . . .'

YES HE DOES! I shout.

Dad locks up the house, pulling on his coat and starts to follow me as I make a run for it towards the postbox, and then past the bench, as Mum stops to hold her side, abandoning her flip-flops so she can run faster. Dad catches up with me at the bus stop, and we run together past the church, turning right into Parks Road.

Dad stops to catch his breath, pushing me onwards. 'I'm right behind you son.'

I sprint towards the museum, spotting Mr Hadfield with a torch on the front lawn, waving and pointing.

'Over here!' he calls. 'He's over here!'

I hop over the footprints, and as I get to the doorway I see him, huddled inside his dressing gown, crumpled in the corner by the big oak doors.

I'VE GOT HIM! I yell back towards Mum and Dad who are

MY GENERAL STATE OF MIND

OVER THE MOON
SUNNY
CALM
OK
PHEW
NOT OK
ALARMED
NEED CAKE
STORMY
BLACK HOLE OF DOOM

running across the lawn.

'I was just shutting up when the little fella gave me a right start!'

Dad picks him up, hugging him tightly, as Mum grabs his face and kisses it. And then does the same with Mr Hadfield.

'Oh thank goodness.' She starts crying, stroking Fred's hair. 'Don't ever do that again! NEVER EVER NEVER!'

He sleepily looks over Dad's shoulder at me. 'He comes alive at night . . . I was going to bring him home.'

'That's it. Mum's planning a holiday!' she declares. 'We need FAMILY O'CLOCK.'

'Thanks, Mr Hadfield.' I shake his hand.

'That's all right, young fellow-me-lad,' he says, passing me one of Fred's slippers. 'Here, he dropped this. I was just like him when I was young. Loved dinosaurs.'

'WAIT!' cries Fred. 'Put me down!'

He walks up to Mr Hadfield, taking his hand. 'Can I see him one more time, Mister Bushy Eyebrows?'

'Oh darn it, I'll be leaving soon anyway,' he says,

pulling out his keys. 'We'll have to keep the lights off, mind. Don't want to go attracting attention.'

Mr Hadfield unlocks the huge wooden doors with a multitude of jangling keys and lets us inside. In the silence I can hear myself breathing and our footsteps echo off the stone floors as we cross the hall. Mr Hadfield's torch searches out the whale skeleton hanging from the ceiling, and the stuffed badger which looks even freakier at night time (if that were possible).

'Here we are.' He switches on a spotlight.

Rory is now bathed in green light, his teeth-shadows projected on to the walls at twice their size, never looking more like he might just come to life. But Fred isn't scared as he dashes over to hug Rory's bony leg.

'Thanks, Mr Hadfield,' I whisper. 'It means a lot to him.'

'No problem. Here, I've got an idea.' He hands me his radio. 'Hide behind Rory—I'll use the other radio at reception. Make sure you press this button so I can hear Fred's questions.'

I duck down behind the T-rex plinth as he heads back to where Mum and Dad are waiting.

The radio crackles with static and then—

'GOOD EVENING, FRED!' comes a voice that sounds exactly how you would expect a T-rex to sound if it could talk with Mr Hadfield's voice over a radio. Kind of a bit gruff and growly, with a hint of posh, echoing off the stone walls.

'Rory!' shouts Fred excitedly, jumping up and down. 'I knew you could talk!'

I can just see his little face lit up with wonder. 'I'M READY TO ANSWER ALL YOUR QUESTIONS!'

But suddenly the doors bang open.

'What's going on?'

It's Mr Banner with a mad-looking face.

'What are these Foxes doing here?
They're banned, Mr Hadfield, banned!
How dare you allow them on the premises!'

'It's not his fault,' I blurt. 'Fred wanted
to see Rory one last time. Blame us.'

'I already do blame you, boy!'

'Now hang on a minute!' Dad rushes over.
'I want a word with you, Mr Banner—'

'Whatever you have to say, you can say
to the police!' He storms over to reception,
picking up the phone. 'How do I get an
outside line on this thing? Where's Mary
when you actually need her?'

'Mr Banner this will only take a few
minutes,' Mr Hadfield pleads. 'And then if you
still want me to call the police, I will.'

'This is nonsense!'

'Sit down with me!' calls Fred, tugging on his
arm and pulling him over towards Rory. 'He comes
alive at night! He's going to answer my questions!'

'What you need is a good dose of reality,'
Mr Banner tuts, folding his arms.

'FRED ALWAYS HAS TIME FOR ME,' crackles the radio again. 'HE SITS BENEATH MY FEET AND ASKS QUESTIONS EVERY TIME HE VISITS.'

'I haven't got time for larking about Mr Hadfield.' Mr Banner shakes his head.

'But I do ask him questions!' Fred beams, plumping up his dressing gown like a cushion and settling down. 'Would you like one of my crisps, Rory?'

'I'M ONE OF THE LARGEST MEAT-EATING DINOSAURS THAT EVER LIVED, SO ONLY IF THEY'RE TRICERATOPS FLAVOURED.'

'How long is this going to take?' The museum director looks over at Mr Hadfield, but Fred has only just got started.

'Who would win in a fight between you and triceratops?'

'WELL OF COURSE I WOULD SAY ME! MY BITE WAS THREE TIMES GREATER THAN A GREAT WHITE SHARK AND I COULD CRUNCH THROUGH BONE! NO CREATURE THAT EVER WALKED ON EARTH HAS BEEN ABLE TO MATCH MY IMPRESSIVE CHOMPING FORCE.'

'Could you fly?' Fred asks, leaning back on Mr Banner's legs so he can see all the way up to Rory's head. Mr Banner has to steady himself on the cabinet behind.

'NO, BUT I HAVE DISTANT RELATIVES WHO CAN. MY BONES ARE LIKE HONEYCOMB INSIDE, JUST LIKE BIRDS', AND ALL BIRDS DESCENDED FROM DINOSAURS LIKE ME! EVEN ROBINS—CAN YOU IMAGINE?'

'Did you clean your teeth?' Fred's in his element, as Mr Banner puts his hands in his pockets, watching my brother and Rory.

'ALAS, MY ARMS WERE TOO SHORT. WHICH MEANT OLD BITS OF MEAT GOT STUCK BETWEEN MY GNASHERS. I HAD ALARMINGLY STINKY BREATH.'

'But you've got teeth the size of narnas, haven't you Rory? Please don't use them on grumpy Mr Banner.'

'MR BANNER ISN'T GRUMPY, FRED. HE'S JUST TRYING TO MAKE THE WORLD A BETTER PLACE. ALL THAT'S LEFT OF ME IS FOSSILS AND FOOTPRINTS. DINOSAURS COULDN'T HAVE

FORESEEN WHAT WAS COMING TO WIPE THEM OUT, BUT HUMANS CAN.'

'Then it's even more important you're still around to teach us a thing or two, Rory,' I say, standing up and walking around. 'Because isn't the future all about upcycling, Mr Banner?'

'Well, yes, of course, one of many things.' He looks over at me.

'So in a way, you'd be saving the planet if you kept Rory. And Mr Hadfield.'

'Things do have to move on, young man.' He flattens back his hair. 'Change is necessary.'

'But sometimes you can use what's right in front of you, if you just reuse it in a different way.'

'I got one more question!' shouts Fred, making us all jump. 'What *DID* you use those tiny stupid arms for, Rory?'

'THEY WERE COMPLETELY USELESS IF TRUTH BE TOLD. BUT IF I COULD, I WOULD BEND DOWN AND SHAKE YOUR HAND, AND MR BANNER'S, FOR ALLOWING ME TO HAVE SUCH A GLORIOUS TIME IN YOUR MUSEUM.'

'Oh, well, um, thank you.' Mr Banner clears his

throat. 'Right, time's up!'

'I don't want you and Mister Bushy Eyebrows to leave.' Fred wipes his nose on his sleeve. 'Please stay.'

'I WISH I COULD. I HAVE SO MUCH MORE TO GIVE—THE STORIES I COULD TELL ALL THOSE YOUNG CHILDREN. YOU WEREN'T THE ONLY ONE WHO SAT AND TALKED TO ME, FRED. HUNDREDS HAVE OVER THE YEARS. EVEN STANLEY.'

'Really?' I whisper, wondering what I could have possibly asked a dinosaur.

'I'LL MISS YOU, FRED. BUT REMEMBER, I WAS ALWAYS LISTENING.' His last word reverberates off the glass roof.

I turn off the radio as Mr Hadfield walks back over, Mum and Dad following behind.

'Did you still want me to contact the police, sir?'

'Ahem, no need.' Mr Banner pats Fred's hair, then pulls a face, wiping his hand on his tie. 'I can let it go this time.'

'Does this mean we're not banned?' I ask hopefully. 'I'd love to come and see the new exhibition.'

'Um . . .'

'Mary can keep a lookout,' Mr Hadfield assures him. 'She may not know all the newfangled facts, but she knows everyone that comes through those doors.'

'Oh I suppose . . . but any more damage and you're out for good.'

'I promise we'll be no trouble,' I squeak, realizing I can't promise anything with Fred for a brother. Fred who's now clinging on to Rory's lower leg for dear life.

'Come on, we've got our memories.' Mr Hadfield takes his hand and leads him away, winking at me.

'Did I really ask Rory a question?' I say.

He stops and turns around.

'Oh yes. The same one your brother always asks. Did you die because all your skin fell off, and I used to tell you—'

'OK, that's enough questions now. I have spreadsheets to finish!' Mr Banner interrupts.

'Thanks anyway, Mr Banner.' I shake his hand.

'What for?' he frowns.

'For listening . . .'

I've realized we can do no more. And as we leave through the big oak doors, I hear a mumble.

'Goodnight Rory,' whispers Mr Banner.

I sleep with the bedside lamp on, so I can keep an extra close eye on Fred. I can hear Mum and Dad downstairs arguing about Gran.

'She's not to be trusted,' Mum says. 'If she'd just kept him on the scarf . . .'

'I know she's over the hill, but if he didn't know the way to the museum, he would have got lost,' Dad replies. 'We might never have found him.'

'Oh good grief! You're right . . .'

'Gran's not over the hill,' I whisper. 'She's still on the hill having a fruit-based cocktail.'

Then Fred blasts me with a silent but deadly. The Classic Egg. And I wish I was on the hill with her.

⤷ COMMON MULTIPLES

Today is the grand opening of the museum's new exhibition and we're on a proper family outing. No scarf this time, as Fred leads the way, giving us a guided tour of the route.

'That's where I can fit six of my bums!'

'With room for my big one!' chips in Gran.

'And right there's where I run out of puff,' he points, before getting us all to do the stepping-stone footprints across the front lawn of the museum. Even Mum in her flip-flops.

A queue of people are snaking through the oak doors. Eventually we climb the steps and reach reception.

'Morning boys! I've got a brand new quiz today! Fill it in to get a carbon footprint sticker!'

I guess you don't know what you've got till it's gone.

'I drawed a picture of Earth.' Fred stands on his tiptoes, handing her his poster, though in all honesty it looks like it's already been destroyed by climate change.

'Ooh lovely!' squeaks Mary. 'Here, have a sticker!'

We walk into the grand hall and before us sits an enormous slow-spinning globe.

'Wow!' we both say together.

It's surrounded by interactive stations, with lots of buttons to press, so Fred immediately starts pushing them all. I press one and make the Earth light up with endangered animals.

'Look Fred! GREAT WHITE SHARKS! If we don't stop hunting them for, quite frankly, no good reason at all, they'll be extinct like Rory.'

'All their skin will fall off?' Fred gasps.

'Something like that, yeah.'

There are hands-on experiments and things to make. I spot Jess creating a bag out of a T-shirt,

MY GENERAL STATE OF MIND

OVER THE MOON

SUNNY

CALM

OK

PHEW

NOT OK

ALARMED

NEED CAKE

STORMY

BLACK HOLE OF DOOM

while Gemma studies mini terrarium gardens.

'Isn't this cool?' Liam appears at my side, scoffing crisps. 'Not sure I understand it, but it's cool. What you reck Fred-bro, you like it?'

'I do. But I a bit don't,' he frowns. Then dashes off, running in circles around the terminals, pressing all the buttons one after the other, over and over again.

Flossie tugs my jumper: 'I don't think he should be doing that, me hearties.'

'No . . .' I try to catch him, but he's too fast, dashing in and out of people, bashing the buttons, until lights start flashing on the globe and an alarm starts to sound.

'WARNING! WARNING!' an electronic voice booms out of the speakers. **'GLOBAL WARMING AT CRITICAL LEVEL!'**

The Earth is glowing orange with forest fires, the seas start to rise, hurricanes whip across the globe, and thick clouds build into a swirling mass. People are pointing at the Fred-Tornado as Dad tries to grab him but the only thing that will stop him is human-sized fly paper (note to self: add it

to my DAY-OUT-WITH-A-BRUV SURVIVAL KIT
if it actually exists).

'FIVE SECONDS TO CATA-STROPHIC CLIMATE CHANGE!'

'OH. MY. GOD! What have you done?' I shout, putting my hands over my ears. 'We've only been here six minutes and you've broken Earth again!'

This is an out-and-out ban if ever I saw one.

'It isn't climate change we've got to worry about, it's Fred!' laughs Gran, as the countdown begins.

'FIVE... FOUR...'

I hear the crackle of a radio.

'I'M ON IT, EAGLE EYES, OVER!'

'THREE... TWO...'

Mr Hadfield rushes in, flips up a lid at the base of the globe, and presses a large green button.

The alarm stops, the chaos dies down, and the lights stop flashing.

'All taken care of.' He winks at me as I breathe out. 'Just reset Earth to avoid disaster. It's supposed to reach critical mode gradually over six months. But your

OVER THE MOON

SUNNY

CALM

OK

PHEW

NOT OK

ALARMED

NEED CAKE

STORMY

BLACK HOLE OF DOOM

MY GENERAL STATE OF MIND

brother sped up climate
change in mere seconds.'

'Doesn't surprise me at all,' Mum says.

'You're still here, Mister Bushy
Eyebrows!' Fred runs over and hugs him.

'I am indeed. I have a new and very
important role. Now what say we pay a visit
to the brand new coffee shop?' he suggests.

'Good idea. Get Fred as far away from Earth
as possible,' I say. And me from the stuffed
badger which is still on display and eyeing
me up ominously.

'Are there 'licious pastries?' Fred
asks, taking Mr Hadfield's hand.

'I can personally recommend the
almond croissant, the Danish swirl, the
apple turnover, and the custard slice.'

He's got my attention now, as I follow them
through to the rear of the museum where it now
spans out into a large conservatory. A large conservatory dominated by a great imposing skeleton.
Because there stood in the middle is—

'ROOOOOORRRRRRYYYYY!'

Fred flings his arms out and runs towards him.

'Welcome to our newly designed **FOOTPRINTS CAFE**, where you can dine with the dinos!' announces Mr Banner, who is already there with some photographers. 'Yes, we decided there was room for all in our amazing museum—our prehistory and our future, existing happily side by side!'

Amongst the tables are dinosaur fossils stood on plinths, and hung up on the wall are the foot-print-covered sheets (including the king-size bed sheet Liam's mum's been looking for).

'We've upcycled Rory!' Mr Banner invites the photographers to take pictures. 'Brought the dinosaurs right up to date in a forward-look-ing way! As a wise man once told me, dinosaurs couldn't have foreseen what was coming to wipe them out, but humans can. We must leave the right footprint behind to save ALL our endangered species. So we gave Rory a good clean up, and moved him—'

'ACTUALLY,' booms Rory. 'I CAME ALIVE AT NIGHT AND MOVED IN HERE MYSELF!'

OVER THE MOON

SUNNY

CALM

OK

PHEW

NOT OK

ALARMED

NEED CAKE

STORMY

BLACK HOLE OF DOOM

MY GENERAL STATE OF MIND

'I knew it!' yells Fred, jumping up and down.

'Why don't you ask Rory a question, young Fred?' Mr Banner urges, inviting over the photographers. 'Did you die cos all your skin fell off?' he asks, sitting on a pile of cushions.

'LET ME TELL YOU A STORY . . .' comes a booming voice, and I notice Mr Hadfield has disappeared.

'Come and sit down!' squeals Fred, pulling my hand.

I squeeze next to him and he leans his head on my arm.

'Here you go my little turkey-vultures.' Mum puts a plate of pastries on our laps, and sits behind us supping her cappuccino.

I lean back and look at Rory as he tells his story, gazing up through his ribs into his huge jaw, teeth the size of narnas, while I tuck into an apple turnover. Science at one end, dinosaurs at the other. Plus flat cake. It's a win-win.

'I'm full of joy,' Fred says, spiffing crumbs. 'I will cuddle Rory till I'm an old grandpa.'

He's about to give me a cuddle too, with a face full of snot and crumbs, until I hold up my hands.

'Tissue?' I suggest. Because I've finally solved snot-shoulders by stuffing his sleeves so full of tissues he looks like he's been working out.

He rubs the tissue all over his face, looks up at me, then wipes the same tissue all over MY face, so I'm left with more crumbs than before, plus damp snot just for good measure. Think I preferred it on my shoulders.

'There's still a place in this world for dinosaurs,' says Mr Hadfield.

'Too right,' Gran agrees. 'We're not over the hill, we're still on the hill grabbing life by the hands and not letting go. Now look lively, Mr Hadfield, you've got more questions to answer.'

A crowd of children have gathered on the cushions, sat waiting for Rory to come back to life again.

'Did I really ask Rory a question?'

I look up at Mr Hadfield.

'Indeed you did. The same question. Every single time. *DID YOU DIE BECAUSE ALL YOUR SKIN FELL OFF?* And I used to tell you—'

'That sixty-five million years ago an enormous meteorite crashed to Earth,' I recite. 'It filled the air with so much dust it blocked out the sun. The plants died, then the plant-eaters died, then the meat-eaters died.'

'You remembered!' Mr Hadfield's bushy eyebrows lift in surprise. 'And you were so obsessed with that story, I had to point you in the direction of our meteorite.'

A memory flashes back to me. I'm a small-year-old pressing my thumbs into the dimples of the metal rock, while Mr Hadfield's warm voice explains *'IT'S FOUR AND A HALF-BILLION YEARS OLD. IT'S AS OLD AS THE EARTH. FROM WHEN THE SOLAR SYSTEM BEGAN.'*

'It was *YOU!*' I exclaim, leaping to my feet. '*YOU* got me interested in space! I can't thank you enough, Mr Hadfield.'

'Just doing my job.'

Then Gran nudges him.

'Oh yes, and I hope you don't mind, but I brought this along.' He reaches behind Rory's plinth and pulls out a package. 'Your Mum mentioned you'd always wanted one, and well, it was only gathering dust in the loft. Would you like it? As a thank you for helping upcycle me?'

'Would I like it?' I repeat, my voice wobbling a bit as I take out the telescope and turn it over in my hands. 'I'd love it, Mr Hadfield! Thank you! At least let me give you my pocket money.'

OVER THE MOON

SUNNY

CALM

OK

PHEW

NOT OK

ALARMED

NEED CAKE

STORMY

BLACK HOLE OF DOOM

MY GENERAL STATE OF MIND

'No need. I've agreed to pay him in cake,' Gran winks.

My eyes and nose start leaking, so I grab one of Fred's tissues from up his sleeve.

'Now you can show us your universe, Stanley,' Mum smiles. 'Unless EastEnders is on.'

'And I honestly won't cover it in bogies.' Fred looks up at me and I almost believe him.

'Oh, one thing you COULD do for me,' Mr Hadfield leans in to whisper. 'Leave the crayons at home from now on, eh?'

'All under control.' I blush. **LEVEL TWO**.

But actually, who knows when Fred will next delight me with his crayons of doom or his Wee Willie Winkie impression? You can't always understand everything, not even with diagrams. Sometimes you just have to accept you're complete opposites, like the different ends of a museum with only Mr Hadfield in the middle.

'Hey! I know our common multiple!' I shout out loud to a bemused Fred. 'It's Mr Hadfield! He got you into dinosaurs and me into space by telling us stories beneath Rory!'

'Common what?' Gran snorts as she sits down for a cup of tea. 'I was one of eight—we had our differences, but there was one thing that bound us together. We were Foxes. And you're Foxes too. That's all there is to it!'

I guess we ARE brothers.

They say we're all made of stardust. But it isn't just that. Somewhere in there is love too.

COMMON MULTIPLES OF STAN AND FRED

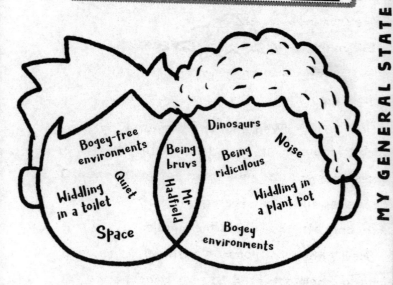

OVER THE MOON

SUNNY

CALM

OK

PHEW

NOT OK

ALARMED

NEED CAKE

STORMY

BLACK HOLE OF DOOM

MY GENERAL STATE OF MIND

And in the end that's what
holds you together.

Well, that and bogies.

SLICES OF THANK-YOU TO

JULIA CHURCHILL—you are an Agent Fairy Godmother and I love you in a non-stalky way

Book sorcerers **ELV MOODY, KATHY WEBB** and **LIZ CROSS**; design magician **HOLLY FULBROOK**; and all at **OUP** for your lovely welcome and finding the perfect match in picture wizard **CHRIS JUDGE**

HARRISON FORD for being Indiana Jones and Han Solo

MR BRENNAN and MR CHAMBERLAIN for making English a joy (and not a subordinate clause in sight)

THE OXFORD UNIVERSITY MUSEUM OF NATURAL HISTORY for Stan the T-Rex, the meteorite, and letting kids touch stuff (though not the wasp nest)

GEORGE & ALEX, without whom these pages would be empty. As would my life. Empty of socks & laughs & hugs & trainers & Marvel stuff—love you to the radiator and back

MUM & LAZ for your unwavering support, love, grandparenting, posh biscuits, and legendary BBQs

KAS for putting up with my tales since knee-high socks, emailing me author rejection stories when I needed them, and being even more excited than me (and I'm pretty darn excited).

PAUL for reading this squillions of times, making me laugh, and generally being lush. Maybe I did look in the mirror first ...

ABOUT THE AUTHOR

I live in Oxford with my husband and two sons
and am often found either looking up at trees
or stars. At school I filled my books with stories
instead of maths, which is probably why I only
just about passed some A Levels. In my teens
I could have become a champion cha-cha-cha
dancer, but preferred to watch TV instead. And in
the world of work I stood at many photocopiers,
dreaming up characters while the multipage
double-sided document jammed in the paper
feeder. Luckily I redeemed myself by learning
to type at almost the speed of light and finally
knuckled down to some writing.

ABOUT THE ILLUSTRATOR

Chris Judge is an illustrator, artist and children's picture book author from Dublin, Ireland. Chris has published several picture books since 2011 and illustrated several texts including the **DANGER IS EVERYWHERE** series with David O'Doherty and Roddy Doyle's latest children's book **BRILLIANT**. He also makes the **CREATE YOUR OWN ADVENTURE BOOKS** with his brother Andrew.

Interesting facts: Chris used to play the bass guitar in a band called **THE CHALETS** many years ago and he is allergic to carrots.

Ready for more great stories? Try one of these...